Paths of Darkness

Michael Subjack

"A Life in Nightmares" was originally published in The Sirens Call Issue #39

Cover Illustration by Martina Moreno

*Dedicated to my friends and mentors Mac Nelson and Eric Sherman
and my cousin Gregory Humm*

I miss you guys.

The Paths

Lucifer's Folly

It was Saturday night and Lucifer had a hankering for a fresh soul. He brought himself up to Earth donning a slim-fitting black suit made of fine silk that he accented with a blood-red tie and matching pocket square. His jet-black hair was slicked back so not a strand was out of place and his coal-colored eyes flickered with glee and mischief. The town he was in was small, depressed, and long forgotten by civilization. As Lucifer danced along the cracked sidewalks of this once-prosperous place, he marveled at the despair that surrounded him. These towns were never as exciting as New York or Los Angeles but they were still a hotbed of desperation, a veritable feast of broken souls. Lucifer would happily explore those other lost causes another time. For now, he had his target picked out. He had been eyeing this particular sad sack for months. The man was sure to be an easy mark and not up to Lucifer's usual standards but again, it was Saturday night. He just wanted to have some fun. And in these situations, Lucifer reasoned that everybody won when it came down to it. The mark would get success and happiness beyond their wildest dreams (albeit for a limited time) and Lucifer would acquire a soul. Win-win.

Tonight's mark was named Eddie Herman. He had been an aspiring video game programmer once upon a time and he wasn't without talent. However, cracking that field was easier said than done and although Eddie had given it the college try, he was never able to gain a foothold in it. He ended up taking a job as a computer technician at a local mom and pop business. The pay was meager and the work was well below Eddie's abilities. It was another sad tale of wasted potential. As bad as that was, it wasn't enough to completely break Eddie's spirits. While ennui had set in, Eddie still had the love of his girlfriend Shauna, a vibrant and pretty girl eager to shake off the shackles of small-town life. And she thought Eddie was the man to help her achieve that lofty goal. While she had stuck with Eddie for six months after he admitted defeat in the fiercely competitive world of video game programming, she began to realize he was not going to be her ticket out and dumped him unceremoniously over text. Eddie completely bottomed out after that. He began drinking heavily and lost his job at the computer store. He was forced to move back in with his mother and stand by as Shauna was gallivanted around town by Mario Monticello, the owner of a popular Italian restaurant. Mario had dreams of expanding nationwide and was on track to do so, giving Shauna the way out that Eddie was no longer able to provide.

Lucifer reached Mario's restaurant (aptly named The Pasta Bowl) and peeked inside. He saw Mario, overweight and varnished with sweat, leading a sing along to Frank Sinatra's "My Way". Shauna sat next to him, fully made-up and dressed to the nines, her shapely stockinged legs glimmering in the warm lights that lined the ceiling. She stared up at Mario with a look that bordered on worship. Lucifer wondered if the adoring townspeople knew that Mario was a raging drunk with a foul temper. He had threatened Shauna with violence if she ever left him but as long as he was able to provide her with a fresh start, she was all his. At least until later tonight. And depending on how desperate she was for a better life, Lucifer might end this glorious Saturday night with two new souls in his possession. And that sounded just fine and dandy to him.

He continued his spirited jig down the street, turning down a darkened alley. His immaculate, wing-tipped shoes slickly weaved their way around mounds of rotting garbage and broken bottles. It wasn't always glamorous work but the reward more than justified it. He stopped by a dumpster and there lay Eddie Herman in his all of his splendor. "Splendor" maybe wasn't the best word, as Eddie was sporting a ragged beard and clothes that hadn't been washed in several days. While Eddie wasn't homeless, the dumpster in the alley behind Mario's restaurant provided him with a good vantage point of his beloved Shauna. In the previous months, Eddie had gone to the restaurant on the regular and sat alone at the bar watching the love of his life shower her affections on a more prosperous mate. The sight became too much to bear one night and Eddie had made a scene before finally being thrown out by Mario, who went as far to call him a loser. Since that night, Eddie had staked out various hiding spots around the restaurant and drank himself stupid as Shauna dreamily watched Mario swoon through old standards by Sinatra and Dean Martin. It was pathetic enough to make Lucifer feel sorry for him. Almost. He stared down at this sad mess of a man and nudged him awake with his wing-tipped shoes. Eddie raised his head and stared at Lucifer with watery, bloodshot eyes.

"Fuck do you want?" he slurred before taking a swig from the bottle that was wrapped in a wrinkled paper bag.

"Eddie Herman!" Lucifer proclaimed, flashing a grin that displayed a perfect set of almost impossibly long white teeth. "Today is your lucky day."

"Am I going to die?" Eddie asked, his tone flat and emotionless.

"Far from it!" Lucifer said, his grinning growing wider to the point it almost reached his impish ears. "Today's the day your life begins and all your dreams come true!"

Eddie regaled him with a look that suggested he thought Lucifer had lost his mind. It was a look he had seen a million times before and the best part was that said look always contained the slightest traces of hope. And Eddie Herman was no exception.

It was time for Lucifer to make his pitch.

He laid out his offer and to his surprise; Eddie wasn't immediately receptive to it. That wasn't unusual but he had taken Eddie for an easy mark. Maybe too easy. Still, it didn't take a lot of coaxing for Eddie to finally give in and ask the same set of questions that always ended with them relenting their soul to Lucifer. Not the easiest mark but far from his most difficult. That honor still belonged to Anne Rice.

"I get rich, I get Shauna back and you get my soul?" Eddie asked, half to Lucifer and half to himself.

"Simple as that. No strings attached. You'll get ten years on this mortal coil with her and every day will be paradise."

"Ten years?" Eddie mused. "But I'm only thirty-two!"

"You can have ten perfect years or fifty more of whatever it is you call this," Lucifer said. "Your call."

Eddie took another sip from his bottle before letting out a belch so putrid it actually made Lucifer yearn for the brimstone he had spent an eternity inhaling.

"And she'll love me again?" Eddie asked, his hoarse, drunken voice imbued with faint traces of boyish hope.

"Purely and unrelentingly," Lucifer said, reaching into his blazer to produce the contract, its edges flickering and crackling like red-hot coals. "Do we have a deal?"

He held out the contract to Eddie, who hesitated to take it.

"Go ahead," Lucifer coaxed. "You'll have ten years before you feel any heat. Well, not *any* heat. The bedroom might prove to be a different story."

He said this last part with a mischievous, musical laugh that proved contagious. Eddie laughed before breaking into a brief coughing fit that produced chunks of brown and green phlegm that splattered his food-stained jeans. He wiped his mouth off and peered up at Lucifer with the helpless look of a stray dog.

"We'll take care of that, too," Lucifer said assuredly. "Now go ahead."

He waved the contract at Eddie who took it and read it over.

"Take your time," Lucifer said. "But it's all boilerplate."

Eddie nodded and began to pat his pockets for a pen. Lucifer snapped his fingers and produced an old-fashioned quill. While that was partly for aesthetic reasons, Lucifer also just preferred them. The classics never went out of style.

Eddie took the quill and signed the contract with a spiky, crooked signature. Lucifer snapped his fingers again and his own name appeared below that in cursive red flames. Eddie's eyes widened and he dropped the contract like it had reached out and bit him.

"Jesus!" he exclaimed.

"Haven't seen him in a while," Lucifer replied, sweeping up the contract and tucking it into his coat. "So how about it, Eddie Herman? Ready for your wildest dreams to come true?"

He offered Eddie a hand that ended in long, neatly manicured fingernails.

And Eddie didn't hesitate to take it.

When they emerged from the alley, Eddie was wearing a suit not unlike Lucifer's (though the silk wasn't as fine as his, he wanted a little separation between him and his marks) and his formerly blotchy skin had a soft, youthful sheen to it. His hair, which had grown thin and wispy, was now thick and wavy. Lucifer himself was tempted to run his fingers through it. Eddie's wallet was fat with cash and credit cards that had no spending limit. A sleek black Mercedes was waiting for him and Shauna in the parking lot. From there, they would drive to the airport and catch a private jet that would transport them to Paris for a month-long excursion. Lucifer had informed him that after that, the sky was the limit. Eddie had cried at his newfound good fortune, even going as far to hug Lucifer. That wasn't unusual but it always made him a little bit queasy just the same. He had ordered Eddie to go out to the parking lot and wait by the Mercedes. Lucifer would then bring Shauna out, priming her with just the right amount of suggestion. It wasn't magic, so-called pick-up artists would be able to do the same thing without much effort. In essence, his work was done. He just needed to sit back and wait for Shauna to fall sobbing into Eddie's arms and tell him that she loved him and wanted to be with him again. After that, Lucifer would return home, satisfied and in the possession of a brand-new soul.

He couldn't think of a better way to spend Saturday night.

Lucifer entered the restaurant to the strains of Sammy Davis Jr.'s rendition of "The Candy Man". He sang along as he danced toward Shauna, who watched him with a mixture of amusement and confusion. Just five feet away, Mario was laughing and pouring shots for a group of exuberant off-duty police officers. Lucifer realized there might be trouble if Mario saw him working his mojo on Shauna but he could always divert attention if need be. A grease fire in the kitchen, perhaps. And if said fire got too out of control, the whole place could burn down. That would be a nice bonus to what was an already pleasurable evening.

"Hello there, Shauna!" Lucifer said as he sat down on the stool next to her, using one of his long nails to pierce a green olive out of her martini glass.

"Have we met?" she asked him, her eyes twinkling with intrigue.

Lucifer popped the olive in his mouth and smiled.

"We have not. And while I'm sure I'd find your company absolutely sublime, I'm here on a behalf of a friend."

"What friend?" Shauna asked, her tone growing wary.

"Eddie Herman, of course!" Lucifer said, helping himself to another olive.

"You know Eddie?" she asked in disbelief.

"Indeed I do. And he'd very much like to see you."

Shauna cast a baffled glance around the restaurant.

"Where is he?"

"He's outside. He wanted to come in but he's afraid to leave his

Mercedes alone with all these ruffians around."

"Mercedes?" Shauna cried out, practically shrieking it.

From there, it wasn't hard at all. A cockamamie story about Eddie being paid for one of his video game ideas, along with an inheritance from a deceased relative. Lucifer used some mild hypnosis but the prospect of Eddie being rich and successful was more than enough for Shauna to want to go outside and talk to him.

The pitch only took five minutes and once it was over, Lucifer had stood up and beckoned for her to follow. They walked out the back, finally catching the attention of Mario.

"Shauna!" he hollered at her but it was too late.

The next phase in the life of the future Mrs. Eddie Herman was already underway.

Eddie was leaning against the Mercedes with a detached coolness when Lucifer arrived with Shauna. As much as Lucifer wanted to take credit for teaching him that pose, it was all Eddie's doing. He figured Eddie had been rehearsing this moment in his head ad nauseam for months. While the pageantry might look a little hokey under normal circumstances, Shauna was entranced by it. And that was something Lucifer could take credit for.

"Oh, Eddie!" she gushed. "Your friend told me everything! I'm so happy for you!"

Eddie smiled and used a black silk hankie to wipe an invisible smudge off the Mercedes.

"Yeah, things are almost perfect," he said.

"Almost?" Shauna inquired, her voice coy and seductive.

"Well, the money and fame are great but without someone to share it with, it's all kind of pointless."

"Why, Eddie Herman," Shauna said, her eyes dancing playfully. "Are you telling me you're still single, even after this onslaught of good fortune?"

"I am," Eddie replied. "And that's because there's only one woman in the world for me."

Lucifer rolled his eyes. He hated this romantic shit. Couldn't they just make it official so he could get out of there?

Tears swam in Shauna's eyes as she walked toward Eddie, her heels clacking on the pavement in an uneven and hesitant manner.

"After everything that's happened you still want me back?" she asked, her ample bosoms heaving as she started to sob.

"Of course," Eddie said, holding out a crimson-colored rose. "So what do you say? Are you ready to spend the rest of our lives together?"

Lucifer cringed a little when he said that. The statement sounded nice but it certainly wasn't accurate. Would ten years be enough for Shauna? Did it matter? Lucifer was just seconds away from owning Eddie's soul and while this wasn't his best work, it had certainly made for an entertaining evening. He began to dance an excited jig as Shauna walked over to embrace Eddie, making their reunion official.

They were just inches away from each other when the crack of a gunshot sounded from behind them. Lucifer watched in disbelief as Shauna's head exploded in a blast of brains and blood, most of it landing on Eddie's fine silk suit.

Lucifer spun around to see an enraged Mario standing in the

parking lot holding a smoking pistol in his hand.

"Bitch!" he bellowed, spittle flying from his lips. "I told you what would happen if you ever left!"

Shit. Lucifer honestly didn't think he had it in him but his temper and a full day of sucking down limoncellos had finally gotten the best of him. Lucifer looked at Eddie, who was staring down at Shauna's dead body in shock. A chunk of brain matter rolled down Eddie's pants and landed on the pavement with an unpleasant-sounding "plop". Lucifer felt a rippling sensation in his blazer and opened it to reveal the contract dissolving into black ash. Of course that was happening. Lucifer hadn't delivered the most important part of the deal. Eddie and Shauna's relationship hadn't been made official. As he watched the black ash uselessly fritter away, he heard a primal scream and turned to see Eddie running at Mario full blast. Mario tried to get a shot off but Eddie was too quick. He knocked Mario to the ground and proceeded to bash his skull in with a loose chunk of concrete. When Eddie finally finished, Mario's head bore a striking resemblance to the slightly burnt lasagna he served on Thursday nights.

Lucifer took in the chaos that had unfolded around him and was only able to utter one word:

"Jesus."

Eddie looked up at him and grabbed Mario's gun, pointing it at Lucifer.

"You said you haven't seen him in a while, right?" he asked, his face covered in tears and green snot.

"It's been a few years," Lucifer admitted. It seemed like such a trivial question but humans often defaulted to such things when shit had completely hit the fan.

"Well, I'll tell him you said hello!"

"Eddie…" Lucifer began but it was too late. Eddie pointed Mario's gun at his head and pulled the trigger. The sound of the gunshot echoed in the empty parking lot. Had Eddie given him just a few more seconds, Lucifer would have explained that he actually wasn't going to meet Jesus. Murder was kind of a no-no in his eyes and when you also factored in suicide, Heaven generally wasn't your first stop.

As Lucifer surveyed the death that lay gruesomely in front of him, he realized that in a strange way, the evening had been a success. He was walking away with the souls of Eddie and Mario. Still, he couldn't help but feel a little flummoxed. This wasn't the worst thing he had ever seen but it was certainly one of the most unexpected. And add to that, he'd have to see Eddie and Mario once he returned to Hell and suffice to say; it would be a little awkward when he did.

He decided to spend the next week in Los Angeles. His old pal Ryan Murphy had a show in production that he could be a background extra on. It wasn't glamorous work but it certainly beat this clusterfuck.

Lucifer heard a woman scream and knew it was time to leave. He snapped his fingers and disappeared into a cloud of black smoke, leaving a faint trace of brimstone in the air. He cursed himself for letting everything get so out of control. Was he losing his touch? Or were people just getting more unpredictable? Either way, he was profoundly disappointed.

Fucking Saturday night.

Lost and Found

I was eight years old when I encountered the creatures of Stone Canyon. I had learned about them the previous fall from my friend Otis Johnson's older brother Newt (the Johnson family made up for their incredibly boring surname by giving their children the strangest first names possible. The daughter's name was Miracle). Newt had overheard us talking about *Candyman,* a movie that had to be the scariest thing ever made. The main character had a hook and could control bees. Or so we surmised from the box at the video store. Otis' mom had taken us there to rent a movie and we ended up getting *Teenage Mutant Ninja Turtles III.* Years later, I still can't help but feel a little cheated by that.

"*Candyman* isn't scary," Newt said with an indifferent click of his tongue. "It's just some guy with a hook. You guys want to be scared, go to Stone Canyon."

"What's Stone Canyon?" I asked. Newt was seven years our senior and a freshman in high school. An older kid even acknowledging you was a rare treat and I didn't intend to let this golden opportunity slip by.

"Stone Canyon's a state park in Ohio," he answered, already losing interest in talking to us. "And Bigfoot lives there."

"What's Bigfoot?" I pressed. It wasn't just having an older kid talk to me at this point; I was genuinely interested in what Newt had to say.

"Bigfoot's like this giant ape that hides in the woods. He leaves these huge footprints wherever he walks, hence the name Bigfoot."

"Apes aren't scary," Otis said. Now it was his turn to be indifferent.

"You're telling me that if you saw a big hairy thing that was like eight feet tall standing in front of you, you wouldn't be scared?" Newt asked his younger brother, knowing full well what the answer was.

"You didn't say it was eight feet tall," Otis replied. His indifference was gone. The thought of such a beast scared him, as it did me.

"People disappear there all the time," Newt said, his interest returning now that he could see he was scaring us. "And supposedly they like to eat little kids. So why don't you guys go there and find out?"

And with a mock spooky laugh, Newt took his leave, his footsteps disappearing down the hallway. We heard his bedroom door close followed by the blaring of Nirvana. I looked at Otis and he looked at me.

"He's just trying to scare us," Otis said, dipping his hand into the popcorn bowl before offering me some. I took a few kernels but I wasn't very hungry. My thoughts and dreams that night would be invaded by giant ape-men that had an appetite for small children.

And a mere few months later, I got to experience the real thing.

It was the summer of 1994 and Otis and his family were visiting relatives in Myrtle Beach. Since he was my only friend, that meant I was kind of up the creek until he came back the following month. But my mom had other plans.

"Tina, how would you like to watch Harold this summer?"

And yes, my name is actually Harold. The fact I had only one friend as a kid is probably starting to make sense to you.

"Oh, come on, Mom!" Tina whined over a breakfast of Lucky Charms and buttered toast. Tina was four years my senior, making her twelve. She was set to go into seventh grade in the fall and spending the summer with her friendless eight-year-old brother sounded about as appealing as a trip to the dentist.

"I'll pay you," my mother replied, in a very business-like manner.

If you're thinking it was kind of pathetic that my mom had to pay my sister to hang out with me, you're not wrong. It's also kind of embarrassing considering I was sitting at the table with them when this exchange was going on but what can I say? The nineties were a different time.

"How much?" Tina asked. Her interest was appropriately piqued.

"Ten bucks a day," my mother replied. "I'll make it fifteen on weekends."

Tina couldn't believe her good fortune. Ten bucks a day just to drag me to the playground and the Dairy Queen that was a few blocks from our house? That was highway robbery.

"Okay," Tina said, already envisioning the trips to the mall she could take with her newfound riches.

"But it has to be for the day!" my mother said, setting the terms. "You can't take him to the playground for half an hour and then dump him in front of the TV so you can talk on the phone with your friends. Morning until dinner time or no money!"

Tina started to open her mouth to say something but decided to keep it shut instead. It was a good deal, even if she was going to have to work a little harder than she initially thought.

And it proved to be a good arrangement for both of us, at least until that fateful day in mid-July when our lives changed forever.

We were at the playground behind my elementary school and it was getting close to dinnertime. Tina mostly sat on the swings while I climbed the monkey bars and went down the twisty slides more times than I could count. It's amazing when I look back and think about how easy it was for me to occupy my time in those days. That playground was like every other playground in America but to me, it may as well have been Disney World.

The daylight eventually began to wane, casting a shadowy filter on the otherwise cheerful and inviting playground. Tina had given up on the swings and was halfway across the monkey bars when she dropped down, sending up puffs of dust from the cedar chips that covered the ground.

"Let's go, squirt," she said. That had been her nickname for me for as long as I could remember. She rarely used my actual name but that was okay. "Harold" wasn't something I liked to hear spoken aloud in those days (or these ones, for that matter).

We began the walk back home as kids whizzed past us on bikes and skateboards, some of them in the same grade as Tina. She waved and said hello to most of them. My sister had always been popular and well liked. I was shaping up to be the antithesis of that.

We reached the top of our street and that's when the blue car pulled up next to us. The window rolled down and a man about our dad's age poked his head out. He looked friendly. He even dressed in the same style clothes as our dad.

"How are you kids doing?" he asked with a big smile.

"Fine," Tina said, poking me in the back so I'd continue walking.

The man laughed and took his hands off the steering in a manner that suggested "You got me!"

"Don't talk to strangers, I get it," he said. "It's a good rule. I tell my own kids the same thing. And I think you go to school with my daughter Laura."

He pointed at Tina when he said this and a faint trace of recognition fell over her face.

"Laura Kanew?" she asked.

"That's her," the man said, smiling. "And I hate to bug you kids because I know you have to be home for dinner but I was hoping I could get your help."

"With what?" Tina asked and the man's friendly face became sheepish and apologetic.

"Laura's birthday is coming up tomorrow and I got her a puppy."

"Awww," Tina replied. She loved dogs. We both did.

"This little goof ball here," the man said, holding out a picture of an adorable German Shepherd puppy, its bright pink tongue hanging out of its mouth.

"It's so cute!" Tina said, barely able to conceal her glee.

"The cutest," the man said, putting the photo away. "And I don't know how much you know about German Shepherds but they're slippery. The darn thing took off on me as soon as I got it home."

"Oh no!" Tina said. She was normally a reserved and mature girl for her age but cute animals turned her to jelly.

"I've got the police looking for it but then somebody from this neighborhood told me they saw it running in this direction, so that's what I'm doing here. I'm hoping to get it home in time for Laura's birthday tomorrow."

"Well, if we see it, we'll let you know," Tina said, poking me in the back again.

The man offered her a strained smile in return but he wasn't done yet.

"The thing is if I see it, I'm not sure I'll be able to catch it. I twisted my knee playing softball last week and I need a couple of good runners. Are you two good runners?"

This should have been the first red flag for us (well, one of them, anyway). In addition to being named Harold, I was also a portly child. It should have been obvious to anyone I wasn't a good runner.

"So how about it?" the man persisted. "We go around the block a couple of times and I'll even give you twenty bucks each for your trouble. Ten minutes tops!"

I looked at Tina, who still wasn't quite buying it. I was totally on the line, though. Twenty bucks seemed like a fortune. That was more than my mom was paying Tina to watch me.

"We should ask our parents first," she finally said.

The man seemed to think this was a good idea.

"How close do you live?"

"Down the street," Tina said, pointing.

"Can I give you a ride there? Time is kind of the essence here," the man said, unlocking his back doors.

I looked back at Tina, who gave me the okay. We got in the man's car, the backseat littered with fast food wrappers and old napkins.

There was an unpleasant odor in the car, resembling dirty socks and farts. Unease began to creep inside me but as soon as Tina shut the door, the man hit the gas and we were driving down the street in the opposite direction of our house.

"It's the other way!" Tina said, her voice already high with panic.

The man turned around and gave us a wink.

"Just thought we'd take a quick ride around the block first."

Tina looked at me with a fear in her eyes that I had never seen before. We had just screwed up. Big time.

And nobody knew where we were.

Although it felt like we had been driving for hours, it was likely only about five minutes before I burst into tears. I could tell by Tina's face that she'd be joining me soon enough but at that moment, she decided to play it tough.

"Our dad's the chief of police," she said. "He'll have every cop in the state looking for us!"

"Your dad is Chief Morton?" the man asked, glancing at us in his rearview mirror.

"Yes!" Tina replied vehemently, her cheeks turning a vivid red.

"The black guy who looks like Gordon from *Sesame Street* is your dad?" the man asked, a knowing smile appearing on his face. It made him look like The Grinch. "Nice try but I'm not buying it."

Tina sat back against the wine-colored seat, her chest and stomach heaving. She gripped my hand so tightly it turned my knuckles white. It might have been painful but I was too scared to notice.

"Don't cry, son," the man said, turning paternal again. "Do you watch *Sesame Street*? Because I've got a television where we're going. And all the toys and candy you could ever want. Plus I just picked up *Aladdin*. You kids like *Aladdin*, right?"

We loved *Aladdin*. In fact, we had just watched it for the umpteenth time earlier that day in the comfort of our den while we ate peanut butter and jelly sandwiches. In attempting to put us at ease, the man had made our situation feel even more terrible. We didn't want to watch *Aladdin* with him in a strange place. We wanted to watch it somewhere familiar where the people loved you and didn't have to trick you into going with them.

We continued driving until we were out of town. We had never been this far from home without our parents before. I had been crying consistently since the man had taken us and Tina had finally reached her breaking point as well.

"Please let us go, sir," she sobbed. "Just drop us off here and we'll walk home."

"Do you promise not to tell anybody I gave you a ride?" the man asked.

"Yes!" Tina blurted out, thick tears spilling onto her teal shorts.

"Because think of how mad your Mommy and Daddy will be when they find out you got in a car with a stranger. They'll probably never let you go anywhere again!"

I learned later that guilting the victim was a common tactic used by kidnappers and abusers but even back then it didn't have the desired effect. My parents could scream at me to the heavens and ground me until I was forty as long as it meant Tina and I could go home.

"I don't care!" Tina screamed. "Just let us go!"

And her crying became uncontrollable after that. It wasn't long before we were both wailing and shrieking like a couple of wounded animals.

"Shut up!" the man hollered, slamming on the brakes. He turned to us, a maniacal look in his eyes and a thick white splotch of saliva on his chin. "If you don't stop that crying right now you're both going into the trunk and I won't let you out until next week! Do you want that?"

Tina and I managed to reduce our crying to muffled sniffs, which seemed to satisfy him. The crazy look dissipated from his eyes, returning him to his friendly dad form. It was like watching Lon Chaney, Jr. transform into Larry Talbot after terrorizing everyone as the Wolf Man.

"That's better," he said, offering us a grin that suggested he was proud of us. "I can think of a couple of kids that are going to an extra scoop of ice cream tonight!"

My stomach was in so many knots I couldn't imagine taking a sip of water let alone eating ice cream.

But even with that in mind, I still foolishly believed that everything was going to be okay.

It was pitch black by the time we reached the entrance to Stone Canyon. There was a ranger's booth but it was closed and looked it had been abandoned for months. An orange metal barricade held in place with chains and a heavy-duty padlock blocked the main road. The man stopped in front of it and opened his door, prompting the dome light to come on. It cast a muted and sickly yellow glow in our mobile prison, giving our captor an even more sinister ambience as he looked back at us.

"Okay, little guy," he said, pointing at me. "Out of the car."

"Where are you taking him?" Tina asked, holding me even tighter.

"My friend was supposed to be here to let us in but he left early, so we need to get in another way."

"So what do you need him for?" Tina continued, holding me so tightly that I had trouble breathing.

"Because I don't want you kids doing something stupid like running away. Figure if I've got your brother with me, you'll be less inclined to do that. Am I right?"

Tina didn't respond. He was.

"All right then," the man said. "Now move it."

He got out of the car and motioned for me to follow. Between being paralyzed with exhaustion, fear, and Tina's unrelenting grip, I found myself unable to move.

He swung open the door and grabbed me, prompting fresh screams from both of us.

"Shut up!" the man ordered and we immediately did. For as scared as I was, it scared me more to think we didn't have any fight left in us.

He took me roughly by the arm and led me to the back of his car. He popped the trunk open and grabbed a set of bolt cutters before slamming it closed. Although I can't be sure, I think I saw a shovel and a bag of something I told myself years later was lime. But my naïve eight-year-old mind was still clinging to the idea that he'd at least give us ice cream.

He walked me over to the gate and went to work on the padlock with the bolt cutters. He hissed and grunted as he struggled to cut through it. I looked past the barricade and saw only black. What kind of a person would want to live in a place like this?

Unable to face the foreboding darkness that lay in front of me, I turned back and looked at Tina in the backseat of the car, dimly lit by the overhead light. She caught me looking and tilted her head slightly. Although I still believed in Santa Claus at that time, I was able to recognize what she was telling me: Run.

"If you're thinking about running, just remember your sister," the man said, in between gasps and grunts as he continued to work the bolt cutters. "You run, you won't ever see her again."

His words stung and despite the fact I loved my sister more than anything in the world, a tiny part of me *wanted* to run. That's something I can only admit now and I still hate myself for it.

And had it not been for the strange howl that came from somewhere within Stone Canyon, I think I would have. To this day, I still haven't heard anything that remotely sounds like it. There's audio on the Internet that supposedly captures what those creatures sound like but I can tell you from experience, those clips are total bullshit. It's been close to twenty-five years and I can still hear that fucking howl in my sleep most nights.

I know he heard it, too, because he stopped working the bolt cutters and briefly looked up. I sensed hesitation in him, which gave me hope.

"What was that?" I asked in desperate need of reassurance, even if it came from the man who took my sister and me under false pretenses.

"Never you mind that," he said, resuming his work on the padlock. "Just remember big sister. We're on the homestretch, so hang in there."

He gave one final grunt and finally broke through the chains and padlock. They hit the ground with a clanging thud and the barricade opened with a rusty and pained-sounding creak.

It almost sounded as ominous as the strange howl we had heard just a few seconds before.

Almost.

We were back in the car after that. Tina put a reassuring arm around me and although I wanted to ask if she had heard the howl, I didn't dare speak. I could tell our host's patience was at an end. After driving down numerous roads of varying quality and surfaces, the man finally parked in a small gravel parking lot that sat at the foot of a winding, snake-like trail.

"Up and at 'em," he announced, his voice cutting through the dense and eerie silence that seemed to permeate every inch of the strange place known as Stone Canyon.

"Where are we?" Tina asked, her voice wavering again.

"Didn't you read the sign? Stone Canyon State Park," the man answered. "This is where the cabin's at."

"There are no cabins here!" Tina protested. "My dad says the state won't let people live here, you can only hike and camp for short periods and…"

The man's hand pistoned out and slapped my sister across the face. The sound was sharp, almost like a firecracker had been set off. Tina and I froze again. I can only imagine the pain and humiliation she was feeling at that moment.

"I think I've had enough of your lip for one day," he said, his voice low and menacing. "You can forget about the ice cream, little missy. Now move your ass!"

He grabbed a green knapsack from the passenger's seat and got out of the car. We never found out what was in that knapsack, as it disappeared along with the rest of him but I can't imagine it had ice cream or a copy of *Aladdin* inside it. He opened our door and shined a heavy-duty flashlight inside the back seat. The beam was so bright it practically blinded us.

"Come on," he said, motioning for us to get out of the car.

We refused to move and the man let out a frustrated sigh.

"If you want to stay here all night, be my guest. But you'll freeze to death before morning. Meanwhile, I'll be enjoying a nice cup of cocoa in my warm, comfortable cabin. It's your choice."

Neither of us wanted to go with him but the man was right. It was already freezing out. I squeezed Tina's hand as we slowly got out of the car. We stood shivering, our shorts and t-shirts not nearly enough to keep us warm from the frigid, piercing wind.

The man pointed his flashlight beam at the trail.

"All right, my little Ranger Ricks. Let's get walking."

Still clasping my hand, Tina and I started for the trail, the man's heavy footsteps scraping on the ground behind us. I could feel Tina tighten her grip as she picked up the pace. She intended for us to run. To where I don't know. But it seemed like a good idea for about two seconds.

"And you definitely shouldn't run now," the man said. "Because I promise you'll fall and break something. They don't call this place

Stone Canyon for nothing. Plus there are all the bears, bobcats, and mountain lions roaming around. I'm sure they'd love a midnight snack."

He said this last part with a sinister chuckle.

I wanted to cry and beg for him to let us go but I was too tired by that point. And so was Tina. If running was no longer an option, we just wanted to sleep and hope we'd wake up and find out that the whole thing had been a bad dream. A terrifying, traumatizing nightmare that we somehow shared because it was so ugly that you'd need two people experiencing it just to survive it. Yes, that's what we both hoped at that moment.

But our evening was only just beginning.

The trail we were on seemed endless. The prospect of a cabin waiting at the end with toys and candy inside it was becoming less and less plausible. The trail was on a steady incline and my short, stubby legs were screaming after about fifteen minutes. Tina had longer legs than me but I could tell she was tired, too. I had heard that grown-ups slowed down as they got older but there was a spring in the man's step as he led us up the trail. He even started to whistle at one point.

"Almost there, kiddies," he announced. "Hang tough! All the ice cream you can eat is just a short distance away."

We both knew he was lying and that prompted more tears but I don't think he noticed. He continued to whistle, the bright flashlight beam skipping and bobbing on the trail in front of us. It was probably another tenth of a mile or so before the trail leveled off into a large clearing. The moon was only half full that night, providing some light now that we were clear of the dense tree lines. I could make out rock formations that looked like something out of Indiana Jones. They stretched endlessly and maze-like into the distance. I couldn't tell where they ended and the trees resumed. It might have been exciting under different circumstances.

"What are we doing here?" Tina asked. "Where's the cabin?"

And that's when the man began to laugh. There were two sounds from that incident that haunt me to this day. The first was the strange howl and the second was the man's laugh. It was shrill and arrhythmic. It barely even sounded human. I clung to Tina and she clung to me, the realization that something terrible was about to happen had hit both of us like a ton of bricks. And as it turned out, we were right.

But it didn't happen to us.

The man continued his shrill, abnormal laugh before finally getting a hold of himself.

"All right," he said, in between gasps and hiccups. "There's just one more thing and then we'll get to the cabin. You ready?"

We weren't but the man approached us, reaching into his knapsack as he got closer. He was only a few feet when we heard a loud crashing sound behind us. Tina and I screamed and the man quickly pivoted around, pointing his flashlight into the trees that surrounded the trail.

"Who's there?" he called out and to my great pleasure, the bastard actually sounded scared.

The eerie silence had fallen over Stone Canyon again but the reality of our situation was undeniable: We had company.

The man continued to shine his flashlight along the trees but everything had gone still again. The man grabbed me and Tina by our arms and started pulling us along.

"Hurry up!" he said, both of us too scared and exhausted to move.

"Please," Tina managed but the man wasn't having it. Plan A had gone to shit. I don't know what Plan B was and I'm guessing neither did he. We continued walking through the clearing, the strange rock formations looming over us like angry, misshapen giants, furious we were disturbing them at such a late hour.

We were almost to the other side and into the woods again when we heard another strange howl. It sounded different from the first one. This howl was shorter and more high-pitched. And within a few seconds, there were more of them, coming from every possible angle. Tina and I were reduced to shaking and sobbing while the man breathed heavily and continued to swing the flashlight around. The beam was no longer steady and he was barely able to hold it one place for more than a second. At one point, I saw something large and hairy moving through the trees. Or was it just a shadow? Even as an adult, I'm still not sure what I saw. But it scared me shitless.

"All right, listen," the man whispered to us. "We're going to go back to my car and get the fuck out of here."

"And then you'll take us home?" Tina asked, her voice fervent and hopeful.

"Yeah, sure, what the fuck ever," the man said. "Let's just go."

And after that, all hell broke loose.

The man was walking well ahead of us. He appeared to have lost all interest in Tina and me. Under any other circumstance, this would have been a good thing but the strange howls and noises coming from inside the woods were still happening around us in full stereo. At that moment, I knew I'd never see my mom and dad again. Although the thought was too painful for my young mind to comprehend, I took a small bit of solitude in knowing I was going to die with Tina, who refused to let go of my hand, even as the creatures continued their terrifying song and dance. I'll never forget the man's final words as he practically broke into a run as we continued down the trail. He turned to us and uttered three words:

"Oh, fuck me."

What followed after that was complete and total bedlam. I remember a roar that made my ears hurt. I remember Tina screaming. And I remember hearing the thick cracking of heavy wood. The man let out a ghastly scream that made him sound more like a woman than a man. Had everything not been so chaotic and horrifying, I might have found it funny. I heard a meaty thud and his flashlight fell into a bush along the trail, reducing everything to total darkness. The man's girlish screams became weak gurgles and there were more breaking sounds. I realized later those weren't branches I heard breaking but the man's bones. There were more howls after that, one of them louder and more prolonged than the others. Tina and I had no idea what to do or where to go. It was only when we heard something moving behind us that we ran.

The man wasn't kidding about Stone Canyon. It's easy enough to fall in broad daylight and shatter your body on the jagged rocks that line the sides and bottoms of the trails. But fate had smiled on Tina and me as we managed to stay on our feet and not tumble to our deaths. I can't tell you for sure if something was in pursuit of us but it sure seemed that way at the time. We eventually reached the bottom of the trail and saw the man's car in the distance. Even in the moonlight we could see it had been almost torn to pieces with all the windows smashed and two of the doors ripped off.

I was delirious with exhaustion and fear but Tina somehow held it together. She guided me to a cluster of thick brush and we both crawled underneath it, the sharp twigs scratching our exposed arms and legs. We were eventually nestled safely in the hollow of the brush and Tina wrapped her arms around me and rested her head on top of mine. Her breathing was still fast and panic-stricken but as the minutes crawled along, it eventually slowed to normal, helping to calm my jangled nerves in the process.

The two of us sat together and shook, both out of fear and from the bitter cold. The creatures continued their din of howls and yips. We'd occasionally hear the crunch of a heavy footstep nearby or the breaking of a branch but as the evening wore on, it all slowly died down. And once there was silence, we slept.

We awoke the next morning, sore and filthy. I went on a sneezing fit and would endure a nasty bout of pneumonia for the next three weeks. Physically, Tina fared a little better than me but as we grew up, it was apparent her mental scars ran much deeper. We crawled out of our hiding spot and looked around. The day was gray and overcast and the ground and trees were misted with dew. I was so thirsty I began to lick some of the leaves, letting the cool water drip down my throat.

Tina stared at me for a minute and then did the same. We would have looked downright bizarre had anyone seen us but we were both past the point of caring. We started to walk, hoping to find the road that had brought us here. As we left our hiding spot, I happened to look down and see something that sent fresh shivers down my spine. I tried to point it out to Tina but she wasn't having it. She just wanted to go home and to my knowledge, she never saw it.

And I envy her for that to this day.

We didn't have to walk long before we stumbled onto the parking lot where the man's car sat, still a mess of twisted metal and broken glass. A park ranger was examining it; his white Jeep parked to the side with its yellow sirens flashing. He didn't even notice us until we were right behind him. The sight of us made him cry out.

"Jumping Jesus! Where did you two come from?"

Tina answered his question with a question.

"Do you have a phone so we can call our parents?"

The rest of the day was a blur of police officers and emergency vehicles. The ranger had wrapped thick gray blankets around us and put us in the back of his Jeep. Within twenty minutes, a police car and an ambulance had arrived.

While we were being looked over by the EMTs, more police officers pulled up. They attempted to ask us questions but we were no use to them at that point. Too much had happened and we were still processing it. We were taken to the hospital and treated for shock and exposure. Our parents arrived not long afterward; our mother a hysterical mess and our father silent and ashen. He was unable to make sense of what had happened but he was hardly alone there.

They released us from the hospital two days later and we were given a hero's welcome when we returned home. We were lavished with gifts from friends we didn't know we had and the mayor dedicated an entire day to us. Magazines and news outlets from all over the country came out to interview us. We even had a segment on *60 Minutes*, which you might have seen. Ours was the one that aired after Andy Rooney whined about the price of canned soup.

We started school on time and stayed famous through that fall and winter. By the time spring came around, we were old news and that was okay, especially for Tina. While she was my big sister and best friend in the world, it was hard to deny she had changed. And I think I hated our captor for that more than anything else.

The police came to identify him as Thomas Lantham, a former schoolteacher from Tampa, Florida who had been fired for being inappropriate with his students (for lack of a better term). Thomas disappeared not long after that and started working his way up the east coast, living under assumed names in various small towns. They found evidence that suggested he had made nine children disappear before he got to us. And only two of them were ever found. To most people, that's the downside of him disappearing. Most of those families never got peace or closure from what that monster did.

We gave the police our story and they simply assumed a bear or a mountain lion had gotten hold of him. It was the very same fate he had warned us about but my sister and I knew the truth. Something did get Thomas Lantham but it was no bear or mountain lion or any other recognized animal.

Stone Canyon has been a hotbed of activity for the creature known as Sasquatch for over sixty years. Google it and you'll find no shortage of tales and low-resolution photos that purport to confirm the creature's existence. There have also been a number of disappearances there, roughly three a year, though the number has gone up at various points. One year saw seven people disappear and the park was closed to the public. It was eventually reopened and the disappearances resumed, albeit at their more "normal" rate.

I've spent most of my adult life perusing information on Stone Canyon and its most mysterious inhabitants. It makes sense they've chosen that particular place. It's a veritable labyrinth of trees, caves, and rock formations. Several Bigfoot groups have asked me to come speak at their conventions, held everywhere from Willow Creek in Northern California to Fouke, Arkansas (home of the infamous Fouke Monster). I've politely declined each time and when they ask me if I know how to reach my sister, I simply hang up. Tina is no longer Tina. She changed her name in her early 20s and the once vibrant girl who ran around in the summer with neon-colored Band Aids on her legs and elbows has grown into a twice-divorced, withdrawn, and guarded woman who doesn't have much interest in the outside world. We speak once a month on the phone and I see her during holidays but things aren't the same. They haven't been since that day. I never bring it up around her and neither do my parents. And I certainly don't mention the word "sasquatch" around her. It's better that way.

It's been almost twenty-five years since the incident and I don't think I'll ever set foot in Stone Canyon again, no matter how much money Animal Planet and the Discovery Channel throw at me (and they've offered me a bundle). Not because I'm still traumatized. I think my age played a big part in my ability to recover from what happened, unlike my poor sister. No, my refusal to go back stems from what I saw the morning we were rescued. It was two giant footprints with five toes each. And said footprints were far too big to belong to any man. And they were situated right next to our hiding spot. At some point during the night, one of the creatures had either smelled us or heard our labored, frightened breathing. Why it spared us I'll never know but I'm forever grateful. And I feel the best way to show my gratitude is to stay away and not enter their territory ever again, especially with a film crew. They have their place and we have ours.

Who am I to upset that?

Phoenix

The world had its millionth apocalypse and while the heat was bad, the fucking vampire was worse. The man had been holed up in his shelter for several weeks and the internal cooling system had broken down days ago. The sweat dripped from his body like a leaky hose and the grim state of things had made the vampire especially hungry. It never fed to kill, of course. With the man dead; the vampire would have no purpose. And frankly, the creature's presence, though vile and life-draining, had become a part of the man's daily existence. There was a strange sense of comfort in knowing it was there, a constant reminder of days past and those yet to come.

Presently, the vampire was resting with a full belly and streaks of the man's blood drying on its chin. Its almond-shaped eyes were closed and its long, alien fingers were tented neatly on its chest. The man, barely able to move from its latest feeding, watched with distaste as a large bug crawled across the wall. Part of him wanted to crush it and feel the warm insides escape its thick, hairy body, but he was too tired. And as it was, the man didn't even hate the bugs. Like what remained of mankind, they just wanted to survive and had to take it where they could get it. But did they really have to come here?

The thermometer on the wall indicated the temperature in the shelter was currently a balmy ninety-seven degrees. The man's thinning hair was matted against his head and his chest was sore from the heaving gulps of water he took to try and stave off dehydration. He could hear the outside world slowly coming to life again. It was already beginning to repair itself and the man wondered why. The only constants it offered were chaos and disappointment. In here, even with the oppressive heat, bothersome bugs and hungry vampire, there was a predictable consistency that operated like a Swiss watch. And while the shelter was feeble and not especially impressive, it was at least his.

With that small sense of comfort, the man went to sleep.

When he awoke some time later, the vampire was perched directly behind him. It wasn't hungry; just asserting its place. The man looked over to see two more bugs scurrying across the wall. With his energy slightly up, the man ran over and smashed both of them with his fists. They left bubbling, viscous streaks of blood on the wall and a sickly-sweet odor that reminded the man of cotton candy.

"Satisfied?" the vampire asked him.

The man nodded as the wall absorbed the bloody streaks, removing any final trace that the bugs had ever even existed. He found it all rather satisfying. He prepared himself a dinner of lukewarm canned soup and a sandwich made with moldy cheddar and stale, crumbly bread. The food did the job well enough and the man looked over to see that the vampire had shrunk slightly in size and was curled up in the far corner of the shelter. It looked dead, but the man knew better.

With his own belly full, he entered his quarters and went to sleep for the night. Even from behind the walls made from heavy concrete and steel, he could hear the world moving and even breathing as it continued to fix itself. He wanted to be angry, but was too tired for anything other than solace. He let himself bask in the outside world's gentle song of healing and recovery before drifting off into a deep and dreamless sleep.

He came out the next day to find the vampire seated on the couch, looking slightly more energetic and robust. It would need to feed soon. The man checked his own food supply and saw he had almost nothing left.

"Well?" the vampire asked, waiting for his next move.

The man tilted his head and listened to the outside world, still growing even in the face of constant resistance and destruction. If it was down, it never stayed that way for long. He saw more bugs making their way around the shelter and began to think that maybe it was best just to let them have the whole damn thing.

He took a deep breath and opened the door to find that not only was the world better than ever, it was cooler and already had traces of green poking up through the cracked, sun-bleached soil.

"Are we leaving?" the vampire asked.

The man nodded as he pulled on his dependable work boots.

And the vampire, who was always eager to take the easy way out, posed a very practical and reasonable question:

"Are you sure that's a good idea?"

The man took another minute to examine the world that had been nothing but flaming rubble just a few days before and decided that yes, it most definitely was.

"Let's go," he commanded and like an obedient dog, the vampire joined him at the door.

The man felt galvanized knowing that even if this putrid creature thrived on draining the life from him, he was still ultimately in control.

And with that in mind, they set out.

Mercy

Things were bad. That was hardly a first for Rick and Kelly but this time around, their situation was truly dire. They had another two days before they'd be evicted from their rat hole of an apartment and their phones had been shut off three weeks ago. It wouldn't be long before they'd be living out of Rick's dying Honda, a rusting relic from a time when things were at least manageable. At their best, Rick had worked as a gas station attendant and Kelly had been a waitress at Denny's. They were never flush with cash but they were at least able to pay their bills on time and have a little bit left over at the end of each month. Things started to go downhill when the Denny's Kelly worked at closed. Since Rick only worked part-time, that meant losing over three-quarters of their income. When they fell behind on their utility bill, Rick decided to tempt fate by lifting a few bucks from the register at work. It didn't take long for his boss to figure out what was going on and fire Rick in lieu of pressing charges. Rick revealed the news to Kelly somewhat sheepishly as they had both sworn to give up their status as petty thieves when they moved in together. Under normal circumstances, she would have been furious with him but she ultimately accepted the news with resigned defeat. He had just been trying to make the best of a bad situation and save for working at a gas station, stealing was the only thing Rick knew.

They had attempted to find other jobs but their town had been in a steady state of decline since the closing of a furniture factory some years back. The factory had been the town's bread and butter and losing it had been a devastating blow. The town would likely never recover and neither would Rick and Kelly. She had insomnia-inducing visions of them sleeping on the street, their bodies covered with sores and their mouths containing rotted teeth from the meth they'd inevitably become addicted to. They had no family members to fall back on and the few friends they had were dealing with problems of their own.

Rick and Kelly were headed for disaster and there was nothing they could do about it.

And it was almost Christmas.

They were eating at their favorite diner when they first met Mercy Jenkins. Going there had been Rick's idea and Kelly had argued with him, pointing out that the money they'd spend there would almost completely wipe them out. Rick reasoned it was worth it to get a little bit of enjoyment out of life and more practically, they still needed to eat. It had been two solid days since they had eaten anything that wasn't stale crackers. Kelly's stomach had grumbled loudly when Rick pointed this out. Suddenly a roast beef sandwich with crinkle-cut fries didn't just sound good, it sounded essential. Five minutes later, they were on their way to what would probably be their last good meal for the foreseeable future.

Neither of them had much to say while they waited for their food. They mostly just sipped their water and stared glumly out the window where a light snow was falling on the remnants of a town long forgotten. They were halfway through their meal before Kelly even noticed Mercy. She had coughed loudly, which prompted Kelly to look in her direction. She likely would have looked away after that if it weren't for the old woman's appearance. It was so startling and ridiculous Kelly almost laughed. She appeared to be in her seventies and looked like a combination of Little Edie from *Grey Gardens* and Eileen Brennan in *Clue*. Her badly dyed chestnut hair was a frantic mess of frizzy tangles. Strands of paisley cloth were anchored to her hair with bobby pins and both ears were decorated with light blue earrings that bore a striking resemblance to shower curtain rings. As Kelly looked closer, she realized they *were* shower curtain rings. An oversized threadbare maroon sweater drooped from one bony shoulder and her shin-length corduroy skirt had also seen better days. And to cap it all off, Mercy was wearing bright yellow tights that disappeared into faded pink Converse sneakers. Kelly had always thought brightly colored tights looked ridiculous regardless of age but she had to give the old woman credit. She actually pulled it off. It was a bizarre ensemble but one Kelly couldn't help but appreciate just a little bit. She had intended to go back to her meal and non-conversation with Rick after that but there was something else about the woman that caught her eye. It was the ring on her left pinky finger that sported a diamond that looked to be roughly the size of a grape. Kelly nudged Rick's foot under the table to get his attention.

"What?" he asked as he wiped away a splotch of ketchup from his upper lip.

"Check it out," Kelly whispered, tilting her head slightly to the left.

Rick looked over at Mercy.

"The bag lady? So what?"

"So check out the rock," Kelly said, taking another bite of her sandwich.

Rick gave it a quick glance before returning to his food.

"It's probably fake," he said, using his last fry to collect the remaining bits of salt and grease on his plate.

Kelly wasn't convinced, so she kept her eye on Mercy, who was busy nursing a plate of soggy meatloaf. It wasn't until they were almost done with their meal that Kelly saw her reach into her tie-dyed purse and pull out a wad of cash the size of a brick.

"Rick," she hissed, motioning toward her again.

Rick looked over and saw Mercy carefully peeling several bills off the wad. His jaw dropped.

"Holy shit!" he exclaimed.

"Still think her ring's fake?" Kelly asked.

They looked at each other, both of them thinking the exact same thing:

Their ship had come in.

Rick hadn't been much of a thief in his heyday but he still wasn't stupid. Well, not *totally* stupid anyway. He knew going over and just striking up a conversation with the woman wouldn't bear any fruit, so they decided to wait for the perfect moment. It came when she dropped her purse on the ground. Rick leaped to his feet and ran over to pick it up. Kelly was a bit startled by the maneuver. She was hoping they'd just follow her home, give her a knock on the head, and make off with her purse and anything else they could carry. Even if the diner wasn't crowded, there were still witnesses. For as bad as their situation was, Kelly feared Rick had just made it worse. She watched as he bent over and picked up the purse, holding it out to Mercy with a wide grin that looked predatory even to Kelly. She desperately wanted to pay their bill and leave but Rick continued to chat with Mercy, who seemed receptive to what he was saying. Predatory grin or not, Rick wasn't without his charms. He motioned for Kelly to join them, which she reluctantly did. And each step felt like a death knell.

"This is Mercy," Rick announced when Kelly finally reached the table. "She wants us to join her for a piece of pie. What do you say?"

Kelly wanted to say that they were setting themselves up for prison or worse but the place made pretty good pie, so she sat down in the booth next to Rick.

Poor decisions be damned.

Ten minutes later there were fresh slices of pie on the table and the conversation was well underway. Mercy went a little heavy on the drug store brand perfume but it wasn't unpleasant. In fact, combined with the rich smells coming out of the kitchen, Kelly found herself thinking about her maternal grandmother, who had been dead for over fifteen years.

Mercy did most of the talking and she spoke with the cadence of a well-rehearsed troubadour. Kelly wasn't just intrigued by this woman, she was growing to like her and based on Rick's expression, so was he.

"I was married to my Norman for almost thirty years," Mercy explained, lazily stirring a spoon in her coffee. "I actually gave up a great medical practice a year into our marriage."

"You were a doctor?" Kelly asked in disbelief. She immediately regretted saying it like that but Mercy didn't seem to mind.

"Six years," she said. "And I was darn good."

"So why did you give it up?" Rick asked.

"Because I was told we were going to have children," Mercy answered as her cheerful demeanor darkened. And for the first time that evening, things felt awkward. Kelly considered coming up with an excuse for her and Rick to leave but it didn't take long for Mercy's warm and inviting persona to re-emerge.

"After Norman passed on, I was too old to start up another medical practice and I had no desire to remarry but I missed having a companion. That's when I got my Cuddles. After Cuddles, there was Carrot, and then Muffin. Most recently I lost my Cookie."

A single tear dripped down her cheek, which she took her time wiping away. She wasn't embarrassed at all. And why should she be? Kelly recalled her own childhood dog Bella, who her parents had deemed a nuisance before dumping her off unceremoniously at the pound. Kelly had cried for weeks when that happened.

"I love having pets," Mercy said. "People break your heart but pets love you unconditionally. It's a beautiful thing."

She took a sizable bite of her rhubarb pie and red juice dripped down her chin.

"So tell me about you two. Are you married?"

"No, we're not," Rick answered. "But what we've got works. Right, honey?"

Kelly smiled and nodded. Being broke and on the verge of homelessness suggested the opposite but now was not the time to air such grievances.

"Really?" Mercy asked. "Because she's very pretty. Just look at that angelic face and that lovely blonde mane! You should really think about locking that down."

Kelly burst out laughing, catching the attention of the wait staff and the handful of patrons in the diner. She covered her mouth and continued to laugh. Rick was decidedly less amused by Mercy's suggestion.

"Marriage is an overrated institution," Rick said. "Look at you, you were married. Did that matter after your husband died?"

"Rick!" Kelly cried out. She was convinced it was all over now but Mercy stayed cool.

"You're absolutely right. I went from marriage to pets and haven't looked back," she replied. "I'm sorry for drawing any improper conclusions."

"It's okay," Rick said. "It's just…"

He paused and Kelly wanted to scream.

Oh, please don't do this, she thought as her legs began to quiver.

"Just what?" Mercy asked with genuine interest and concern.

"We've hit kind of a bad spot," Rick admitted. "Money-wise."

A low humming filled the air and it took Kelly a few seconds to realize it was coming from her. She stopped when she saw Rick and Mercy staring at her.

"I'm really sorry to hear that," Mercy replied, finishing her coffee. "And at Christmas time. How rotten."

Kelly knew what was coming next. Mercy would slide out of the booth, pay her check, and then disappear into the night, checking her rearview mirror as she went. She'd lock her house up tight and maybe inform her neighbors about the two desperados that tried to shake her down at Wyatt's Diner.

Kelly clenched her fists; suddenly wishing she had never met Rick. He was a complete loser. Why had it taken her so long to realize that?

"Tell you what," Mercy said, standing up and grabbing her purse. "How about I pay the check and the two of you can follow me back to my place?"

Kelly couldn't believe it. Neither could Rick.

"Really?" he asked, his tone incredulous.

"Sure," Mercy replied. "I've got plenty of wine and junk food. It'll be nice to have some company. I've been all alone since Cookie died."

"Yeah, but…" Rick began before Kelly dug her nails into his thigh. He took the hint and shut up.

"We've love to. That's so generous of you," Kelly said, smiling as sweetly as the circumstances would allow. "Do you want us to pick up anything on the way?"

"Cheese," Mercy stated before walking up to the register without another word.

"Cheese?" Rick asked but Kelly didn't bother responding.

Considering what they'd be walking away with, the request sounded more than fair to her.

A few minutes later they were en route to the grocery store to pick up the cheese. Mercy had written her address on a grease-stained napkin and handed it to Kelly, her eyes sparkling with excitement. Knowing how desperate the old lady was for company was a little heartbreaking but Kelly and Rick's situation was far worse. At least that's how Kelly justified it inside her head.

"What the fuck was that back there?" she asked Rick. He didn't respond at first and instead stared out the windshield with grim determination.

"What?" he finally said, his voice so low she almost didn't hear it over the sick rumbling of the car's engine.

"You actually told her we were broke!" Kelly said. "Do you realize you almost blew the whole thing?"

"I couldn't help it," Rick said. "She kind of reminds me of my grandma."

His sweaty face turned red when he said this. Rick was not a sentimental guy.

"Are you kidding me?" Kelly asked. "When we first saw her, you said she looked like a bag lady!"

"Yeah, but once I got talking to her, she was sweet. Like I could tell her anything."

He flushed an even deeper red and Kelly heard the worn leather on the steering wheel creak as he tightened his grip on it.

"So are we not going through with this now?" Kelly asked. "Do we just have some cookies and a glass of wine and tell her good night?"

"No, we'll just get her drunk and once she passes out, we'll clean her out."

Kelly liked it. Simple and safe but there was one thing she couldn't help but ask Rick.

"And you're okay with stealing from somebody who reminds you of your grandma?"

Rick shrugged.

"Considering how I much stole my real grandma, yeah, I'd say I'm fine with it."

Kelly laughed. Even in the worst of times, Rick knew how to make her do that.

It was about the only thing he was good for anymore.

Mercy's house ended up being a little further away than they anticipated. Rick muttered something about not having enough gas to get back to town and Kelly found herself pressing her fingers into the wheel of cheddar cheese they had purchased. She wondered why she was so nervous. Yes, they were robbing an old lady blind but it was going to be done in a way where nobody got hurt. That had to count for something.

They eventually reached a long driveway on the outskirts of town. The numbers on the rusted mailbox confirmed it was her place. The driveway seemed endless as they drove down it and the tall trees surrounding it blocked out almost all the moonlight. Kelly found it a little scary.

"Maybe she's been dead all along," Rick said with a shaky laugh. He was also scared, which helped put Kelly a little more at ease.

They finally reached the house, which was large but not showy. Kelly had expected something akin to the Addams Family mansion but Mercy's place was well kept and fairly modern. Rick gave an appreciative whistle as they parked in front of it.

"Not bad, right? Maybe she'll let us move in!"

Kelly looked down at the cheese, which had become dented and misshapen from her nervously digging her fingers into it.

"So are we going through with this?" she asked Rick. "You're not going to end up sitting on her lap and sucking your thumb, are you?"

"Very funny. We'll keep it relegated to small talk. Just remember to keep her glass filled."

"Sir, yes, sir," Kelly said with a mock salute.

They reached the front door, which had a sign hanging from it depicting a smiling cartoon parrot.

"Welcome to the Jenkins House!" proclaimed the cheerful bubble coming out of its beak.

Rick knocked and Kelly stared at the sign as feelings of self-loathing began to creep around inside her. As she began to wonder if she could still go through with it, the door swung open to reveal an exuberant Mercy, dressed in a garish silk kimono. She had a full glass of red wine in her hand and based on the redness of her cheeks, she was already about halfway to being completely shitfaced.

"Hello, my lovelies!" she announced, her breath rank with whatever sugary wine she was downing.

Kelly didn't know much about wine but she knew a lot of sugar meant Mercy was destined for a pretty nasty hangover tomorrow.

And that wasn't even going to be the worst part of her day.

As they entered the house, Mercy ushered them into the living room. The furniture and overall décor were downright tasteful. Kelly didn't understand how Mercy could have such a bizarre fashion sense but be totally on point with her house and furniture. It didn't gel but then again maybe the husband was the one who did the decorating. Either way, everything in here beat the lumpy, moldy couch Rick and Kelly kept in their soon-to-be vacated apartment.

Mercy motioned for them to sit down before disappearing into the kitchen with the wheel of cheese. She returned a few moments later with a tray that had two glasses of wine on it, along with an assortment of potato chips and hastily decorated gingerbread men cookies.

"Are those gingerbread men?" Rick asked, his voice almost a squeal.

"They are," Mercy said with a wink. "Help yourself!"

"Thanks!" he said, taking one and biting into it like an eager child. "I haven't had one of these in a coon's age!"

Kelly almost choked on her first sip of wine. Nothing like a little casual racism to put a stranger at ease. Mercy seemed okay with it but Kelly was eager to change the subject.

"Where's the cheese?" she asked as she scanned the tray.

"These go better with this wine," Mercy explained. "We'll have the cheese later."

"This wine?" Rick asked. "How much wine are we having tonight?"

"As much as we can handle!" Mercy said vibrantly. "Making new friends calls for a grand celebration!"

Rick gave Kelly a quick glance. This was going to be even easier than they expected.

It took them only fifteen minutes to kill the first bottle. Mercy was such a whirlwind of stories and laughter that Kelly had let her guard down. Her head began to spin and she made a mental note to take it easy for the rest of the night. She asked Mercy for a glass of water and the old lady pirouetted into the kitchen, singing The Beatles' "Rocky

Raccoon" at the top of her lungs.

"I think she'll be passed out soon," Rick said, his words already slurred.

"Are you kidding me?" Kelly asked. "She's kicking our ass! I'm ready to crash and it's only been one bottle!"

"What if she drugged the wine and wants to have her way with us once we're asleep?" Rick suggested. Kelly looked at the dopey smile on his face and realized the idea didn't exactly repulse him. Sex slave for an old lady. Is that how far they had fallen? Or was there just a lot about Rick she didn't know?

Mercy returned with the water and Kelly took a sip. It had a strange metallic taste to it and Kelly wondered if Mercy really was planning on drugging them.

"Well water," Mercy said as she sat down next to Rick. "Sorry. I meant to pick up some of the bottled stuff at the grocery store earlier."

"That's fine," Kelly said, setting them glass down on the table.

"More wine?" Mercy asked, holding up a new bottle.

"Please!" Rick replied, holding out his glass. He looked at Kelly and raised his eyebrows at her. She had no idea what he was attempting to convey but she could feel their plan unraveling with each passing minute. Kelly was ready to cut their losses and leave but Mercy had already poured a fresh glass for herself and Rick.

"Would you guys like to take the tour?" Mercy asked.

"We would," Rick responded before raising his eyebrows at Kelly again. Jesus Christ. She wanted to jam her thumb in his fucking eye.

Do that one more time, asshole, she thought as she watched Mercy and Rick stand up. Although Mercy had no trouble getting up on her own,

Rick grabbed her by the elbow and guided her to her feet.

"My, what a gentleman!" she said, batting her eyelashes at him in an exaggerated manner. Rick laughed and put his arm around Mercy. Kelly wanted to vomit and then leave, not necessarily in that order.

As she watched her boyfriend stumble out of the room with his arm around Mercy, she wondered if that was even possible anymore.

They reached a steep staircase and Mercy groaned.

"I hate these steps!" she whined. "I need more fuel to reach the top!"

She downed her wine and held her glass out to Rick for a refill. Kelly cringed when she saw Rick take two thick swallows from the bottle before pouring Mercy a full glass.

"Thank you, my lovely."

She took a sip and then started up the stairs. Rick went after her but Kelly grabbed his arm. Mercy turned and waited for them.

"You go ahead, we'll be right there!" Kelly said, motioning for Mercy to keep moving.

Mercy shrugged in a manner that said "Suit yourselves" and continued upstairs, her bare feet making muted thuds on the varnished wood steps.

"What is going on with you tonight?" Kelly asked Rick.

He responded by holding up the bottle of wine to her lips and trying to get her to drink. Kelly pushed it away and smacked Rick on the arm.

"This is exactly what I'm talking about! You do remember why we're here, right?"

"Sure," Rick said. "And now she's showing us where everything is. It'll make her cleaning her out that much more efficient."

"Clean her out? You're having trouble walking right now!" Kelly exclaimed.

"I've got a few surprises left in me," Rick said cryptically before taking another sip of wine.

He went upstairs and Kelly couldn't help but think how much he looked like an ape when he walked. What had she ever seen in him?

That was the moment when Kelly decided to take everything and leave Rick in the dust.

Let his new girlfriend take care of him.

When Kelly arrived at the top of the stairs, she found Rick waiting for her, his eyes squinty and bloodshot.

"Everything okay?" he asked.

Everything's fine, she thought. *We're going to rob an old lady and then I'm going to leave you in the lurch and disappear forever.*

"Of course," she said, kissing him on cheek, which was rough with stubble and greasy with sweat. It was like kissing a pig's ass.

"Down here, lovelies!" Mercy called out. They turned and saw her at the very end of the hallway, a frizzy-haired silhouette standing in a doorway that had harsh fluorescent light pouring out of it.

"We're coming!" Rick said, shuffling down the hallway.

Kelly decided it was time to put her in plan in motion.

"Do you have a bathroom?" Kelly asked.

"First door on the left," Mercy said, pointing at a yellow door next to Kelly. Rick joined Mercy at the end of the hallway and now it was her turn to guide him. She put her arm around his waist and whispered something to him. He laughed and took another sip of wine before both of them disappeared into the room.

Kelly shook her head and went into the bathroom. She splashed some cold water on her face and took a look at her reflection in the mirror above the sink. Her face was a little red but otherwise, she looked lucid. And she felt lucid, too. Her plan was to sneak back downstairs and grab Mercy's purse. She wouldn't be getting away with any of the jewelry but the cash would be enough to get her started. She'd take Rick's piece of shit to the bus station and buy a ticket to anywhere that wasn't here. After that, it didn't matter. Kelly was free. It took meeting a drunken old hag to realize just how trapped she had been with staying with Rick. For that, she would always be grateful to Mercy. She even hoped that Mercy could eventually come to forgive her. As for Rick? Fuck him. She no longer cared.

Kelly splashed some more cold water on her face and then gripped the sides of the sink as she prepped herself to make her life-changing maneuver. She was just about to leave the bathroom when something caught her eye. It was Mercy's medicine cabinet. It was half open and Kelly could read some of the labels on the pill bottles inside it. Ketalar. Kelly recognized that as ketamine. While she never ventured past pot or the occasional line of cocaine, she had friends who used it on the regular. She walked over to the cabinet and opened it all the way to get a better look at some of the other bottles. Oxycontin. Lots of oxycontin. And a bunch of other things Kelly didn't recognize. It definitely wasn't aspirin, though.

Kelly's first thought was that maybe it was medicine for Mercy's husband but most of the labels looked brand-new. It was a little unsettling but Kelly wasn't going to worry too much about it.

In just a few minutes, she'd be long gone.

Kelly took a nervous pee and then stepped out of the bathroom, expecting to hear Mercy yammering away while Rick responded with boorish laughter. To her surprise, there was almost total silence. It was so quiet she could hear the ticking of a clock coming from somewhere downstairs.

She wanted to call out for Rick but stopped herself. Whatever was happening, it might make her getaway even easier. She started for the stairs when she heard the door at the end of the hallway creak open.

"Down here, dear!"

Kelly looked back to see Mercy standing in the doorway again, only this time the lights in the room were turned off, making it pitch black.

"I was just going to help myself to some more cookies and wine!" Kelly said, doing her best to sound casual.

"Come down here," Mercy offered. "We've got plenty. And you'll love what I have to show you in this room!"

"Really?" Kelly asked. "Because it looks kind of dark. How am I going to see anything?"

She laughed but it sounded forced and high-pitched. Her poker face was starting to crack.

"It's a video on the computer. It looks best when the lights are off," Mercy said, holding the door open and motioning for Kelly to go inside. Kelly suddenly felt like Gretel and had a bad feeling the witch had already eaten Hansel.

She was about to turn on her heels and run when she saw something that made her scream. It was Rick, half-conscious and drooling. He was attempting to crawl out of the room with a large hypodermic needle sticking out of his back.

"Honest to goodness," Mercy said as she looked down at him with mild annoyance. "How are you still moving? If I give you any more of that, I might kill you! Now as for you…"

She looked up at Kelly, who was already making a break for the stairs. She attempted to take the stairs two at a time, which proved to be a terrible mistake. When her left heel landed, it missed the step and caused her to slip and tumble down the stairs. She landed at the bottom and cracked her head on the hardwood floor. The pain was explosive at first but then reduced itself to a dull throbbing. Her vision was blurred and when she looked up, she saw Mercy standing over her with a fresh hypodermic needle in her hand.

"Well, I can see you're going be a handful," she said as she knelt down next to Kelly. "But that's okay. I like a challenge."

There was a brief pinprick in Kelly's neck and then nothing.

Her weeks-long bout with insomnia was finally over.

Kelly woke up to find herself in a room with cream-colored concrete walls and a puke green tile floor. She had a throbbing headache and Mercy had stripped her down to her bra and panties. There was a shackle locked around her left ankle held in place by a heavy chain about six inches long. Kelly gave it a tug but it was welded firmly to the floor. Short of turning into the Incredible Hulk or finding a blowtorch, Kelly wasn't going anywhere. She took several deep breaths and did her best not to panic. As long as she was still alive, maybe she could reason with Mercy. She'd tell that she wouldn't call the police or let anybody know what had happened. She just wanted to leave town and never come back.

The door at the front of the room opened and Mercy came in carrying a tray with two stainless steel bowls on it. She also had a large photo album tucked under her right arm. Kelly almost didn't recognize her at first. Her hair was tied back in a conservative bun and she wore a plain blue sweater over tan slacks. There were no signs of the oddball Kelly and Rick had met last night. Just an evil fucking monster.

"Feeling better?" Mercy asked her.

"Please," Kelly croaked. "Please let me go. We weren't going to hurt you."

"Oh, I know," Mercy said, setting the tray and photo album down in front of Kelly. She walked across the room and dragged over an old rocking chair. Kelly was already having fantasies of taking off one of the runners and jamming it into Mercy's quirky fucking skull.

"If you're thinking of trying anything, don't," Mercy said, removing a Taser from her pocket.

"I wasn't going to!" Kelly protested. "I'm sure we can figure this out if you just…"

Mercy suddenly reached out and zapped her with the Taser. Kelly's entire body clenched up and her already obnoxious headache flared to agonizing levels.

"I actually had other plans last night," Mercy said, replacing the Taser in her pocket as she sat down in the rocking chair. "And then I met you two."

"Where's Rick?" Kelly asked, still reeling from the shock Mercy had given her. The previous night she couldn't wait to be rid of him. Now she wanted him more than ever.

"Resting," Mercy replied. "He'll need a couple of days."

"A couple of days?" Kelly asked, letting out a choked sob.

"Before he's up and around," Mercy explained. "You're home now."

"This is not our fucking home!" Kelly shrieked, lunging forward but only making it a few inches before the shackle around her ankle violently jerked her back.

"Really?" Mercy asked, not at all startled by Kelly's outburst. "Because it sounds like you two were on the verge of being homeless. I saved you."

"Fuck you!" Kelly spat at her.

"Such language," Mercy sighed. "Here, let me explain."

She bent down and picked up the photo album and began to leaf through it.

"My Norman was a good man when I met him. Or at least I thought he was. It didn't take long for me to realize he had something of a drinking problem and a temper. And he liked to take out his frustrations on me."

She rolled up the sleeve to her blouse and showed Kelly a circle-shaped scar the size of a quarter.

"He did that when I didn't have dinner ready when he came home. And this…"

She lifted up her pant leg to reveal a veiny, white leg with a jagged red scar about six inches long on her shin.

"He did that with a box cutter when I was out with my girlfriends for too long."

"I'm sorry," Kelly said, hoping her sympathetic tone might help let Mercy's guard down.

"All water under the bridge," Mercy said with a dismissive wave. "One night he was on one of his benders and not unlike you, he fell down the stairs. Only it wasn't a nasty bruise and a mild concussion he got. No, Norman suffered severe brain damage."

She recounted this last part with a slight smile.

"At first, I didn't know what I was going to do. My family and friends all told me to put him in an assisted living facility and move on. There was nothing I could do for him and he'd require more care than I could provide, even as a doctor. But that seemed wrong to me. Abandoning him when I had vowed to spend my life with him. In sickness and in health, you know."

She sat back and let out a long sigh.

"The first month was the worst. He didn't have control over his bodily functions; it was difficult getting him to eat, he would get up and wander around at random hours. I almost lost my mind."

Almost? Kelly thought.

"But then something happened. I was talking with one of my girlfriends and she was telling me about a new puppy her family had gotten. I had always wanted a pet but Norman wouldn't allow it. Too much work and too messy."

Mercy stopped to remove a loose thread from her blouse.

"My girlfriend was telling me how the puppy was having accidents left and right, it was fickle about eating, it had run away from her and she spent a whole day tracking it down. I thought that all of that sounded very familiar. And that's when it hit me. Norman was no longer a husband. He was the pet I never had."

Mercy's eyes took on a dreamy look as she continued talking.

"I began taking him on walks, complete with a leash and collar. That way he couldn't wander off. I also found him a food he liked and it just so happened to be Purina. Isn't that funny?"

She laughed but Kelly didn't see the humor in it. At all.

"While he occasionally still had accidents in the house, I found as long as I walked him three times a day, he would do his business outside, just as happy as a clam. And I was happy, too."

Mercy stared wistfully across the room before her expression saddened.

"But he passed on. As all pets do. And for the first time in my adult life, I was alone. But then I decided there was no reason I couldn't get another pet. People replace pets all the time. Why should I be any different? So…"

She held up the photo book to Kelly, revealing an assortment of men and women on all fours and completely nude save for the collars around their necks. A section of their hair had been shaved off and they all had the same ugly scar crisscrossing down their heads with the same vacant look on their faces.

"I've been through so many pets over the years but I just can't help myself."

Kelly didn't hear that last part. She was too busy screaming.

When she finally calmed down, Mercy explained what was going to happen next. She did it in a way that suggested she was sharing a recipe with Kelly and not mutilation and torture. Once Kelly had fully recovered from her fall, Mercy would lobotomize her and then give her the necessary training to ensure she'd be a good pet. And that was it. Kelly would be a drooling vegetable that a psychotic old woman would drag around on a leash. Everything that had happened prior to this had been bad but this was a whole new level of hell. Kelly cried and pleaded with her but it was no use. Mercy had made up her mind.

"I'm just so lonely," Mercy said, squirting out some tears of her own. "And all my pets were so desperate and lost before I found them. Homeless people, drug addicts. I gave them a home and a purpose. And my Cookie…"

She pointed to a picture of herself with a large hairy man. Mercy was seated in an easy chair and the man was curled up in front of her feet like a loyal German Shepherd.

"I loved him so much," she said, more tears spilling down her cheeks. "He was so loyal. He slept at the foot of my bed, he would nudge me when he wanted to be petted. And then he choked on pantyhose."

She let out a harsh bark of a laugh.

"Careless on my part. You think you've left something out of their reach but…"

She shook her head and sobbed briefly before looking at Kelly, her eyes hopeful and desperate.

"But now I've got you two. Twice the love."

She smiled and stood up.

"But get some rest. I want you in good shape for your

transformation."

She started for the door and Kelly began to scream again.

"Let me out of here, you crazy fucking bitch! I'll kill you!"

Mercy looked back at her, nonplussed.

"Eat something and go to sleep."

Kelly examined the bowl. In addition to the dry food, there were also chunks of something rubbery and yellow. It took Kelly a minute to realize it was the cheese they had brought with them last night.

"What the hell is this stuff?"

"Cat food. I thought it suited you. I added the cheese because I've found it helps settle your stomach as you switch over to your new food. If you're going to change a pet's diet, you have to do it gradually."

And then she left the room.

Kelly became dizzy and her throat was sore from screaming. With no other recourse, she collapsed on the floor and began to weep.

After Kelly had finished crying, she slept for a couple of hours. When she woke up, she found the dizziness had subsided and her newfound energy allowed her to think clearly about how she was going to make her escape. She examined the food and water dishes Mercy had left for her. They were both made of stainless steel, too sturdy to be broken apart but too light be yielded as weapons.

And we thought she was going to be an easy mark, Kelly thought bitterly. She had always considered herself much more intelligent than Rick.

Now she wasn't so sure.

The door opened a little while later and Mercy came in with a container of cat food and a bottle of water.

"Good morning, lovely," she said. "It's a beautiful day. I'm excited to get you outside soon so you can see it for yourself."

"You can let me out today," Kelly suggested. "The fresh air would probably do me some good."

Mercy laughed like Kelly had cracked an extremely funny joke.

"You're cute," she said. "But we both know that won't work. The good news is that I think you'll be ready for surgery tomorrow. And then everything will be the way it's supposed to be. How does that sound?"

Kelly fought every urge she had to spit at the old bitch. Instead, she gave her a weak smile.

"That's my girl," Mercy said before glancing down at her food. "Oh, dear. You didn't eat anything."

"That's because it's fucking cat food," Kelly said, allowing her pleasant façade to slip. "I'm not eating cat food."

"But you will," Mercy said. "And you'll need your strength for your transformation."

She dumped some more food in Kelly's bowl and nudged it toward her.

"Eat," she commanded.

Kelly shook her head and Mercy sighed.

"Do you really want to do this the hard way?" she asked Kelly.

"What's the hard way?" Kelly snapped. "Beating me with your girdle?"

"Last chance," Mercy said, unfazed by Kelly's retort.

Kelly shoved the bowl away and stared up at her defiantly.

"Okay then," Mercy said.

She turned around and left the room. When she returned, she was carrying something that looked like a hybrid of a gas mask and a funnel.

"What the fuck is that?" Kelly asked, trying to back away but Mercy was on top of her. She managed to jam the mouthpiece over Kelly's head and fasten it in place. Kelly continued to struggle as Mercy held up the funnel section of the strange apparatus and proceeded to dump the bowl of cheese and cat food down it. Kelly gagged as the bits poured into her mouth.

"Eat!" Mercy ordered and with no other choice, Kelly began to chew the food.

It was awful. The cheesy had become dried out and the cat food had a sickening fishy taste to it. Kelly struggled not to vomit but managed to chew and swallow the food. Mercy removed the mask and Kelly grabbed the bowl of water and drank it down in two quick gulps.

"That's better," Mercy said with the pride of a mother who's just seen her child win a spelling bee. "Now I have to go out but you get some rest. Big day tomorrow."

She poured Kelly some more water and then left the room, shutting the door behind her and locking it.

As humiliating as the experience was, Kelly had renewed hope. She had found her way out of this place.

And Mercy just happened to be wearing it.

Kelly spent the next hour thinking about her escape plan and playing out every possible outcome. As she waited for the old bitch to come back, she prayed her plan would work. It seemed solid but she was also dealing with Mercy. This was a woman whose breed of crazy wasn't just evil it was downright fucking crafty.

Her outfit today had consisted of a faded Beatles t-shirt that she wore over blue and white Zubaz and rainbow-patterned Crocs. The most important part of the outfit were the paisley strips she had in her hair again. Those were going be Kelly's way out. She just needed to bide her time.

Kelly had observed that Mercy's outfit was a stark contrast from what she wore the previous day, which had been plain slacks and a sweater. She saved the oddball outfits for when she went out in public and why not? It made her the quirky, somewhat batty but ultimately harmless old widow who lived on the outskirts of town. Who would believe she'd ever hurt anybody?

Her entire fucking life is a ruse, Kelly thought. *And she's in complete control of it.*

Or at least she was. Kelly smiled as she thought of her escape plan and how she couldn't wait to see the look on the old bitch's face before she bashed it in.

It was another few hours before Mercy entered the room dressed in a blue velour tracksuit. Kelly was struck by a wave of panic when she saw Mercy had changed clothes. She hadn't expected that. She craned her neck to look at Mercy's hair and was relieved to see she had left the paisley strips in. This could still work out.

Mercy poured some fresh cat food into Kelly's bowl before

dropping in some hunks of cheese.

"And how are we doing tonight?" she asked Kelly.

"I'm much better, thank you," Kelly said, reaching for some of the food. She had to make this look convincing. She chewed the awful-tasting food and had to fight every instinct to spit it out but it was working. Mercy was pleased.

"Very good," she said. "Can I get you anything else?"

"Some more water please," Kelly said, holding up the empty bowl. Mercy nodded.

"I'll be right back."

As soon as her back was turned, Kelly spilled the bowl of food. It scattered across the floor at a distance that was too far for her to reach. So far, so good. An exasperated Mercy turned back around.

"Oh, for goodness sake!" she cried out.

"I'm sorry," Kelly said, doing her best to look like a whipped dog.

"Cheese and rice," Mercy huffed, storming out of the room and slamming the door behind her.

The reaction made Kelly a bit uneasy. She had just spilled some dry food on the floor. What was Mercy's reaction when one of her "pets" had an accident? Did she rub their noses in it? She had a vision of Mercy rubbing Rick's face in his own piss and shit and wanted to laugh but couldn't. The whole thing was just too awful.

When the old lady came back a few moments later she was carrying a pitcher of water and a rolled-up newspaper. She poured the water into Kelly's bowl, allowing some of it to slop over the sides.

"You could have at least started to clean your mess up," she scolded.

"It's hard to move with this thing around my ankle and…"

Mercy brought the rolled-up newspaper down so fast it whistled. It struck Kelly in the nose, prompting her eyes to squirt out hot tears as her nose began to throb.

"Bad!" Mercy screamed at her.

Kelly did her best to compose herself as Mercy knelt down and began to sweep up the food with her hands. As she leaned over to dump the food into the bowl, Kelly reached over and yanked on one of the strips in Mercy's hair. The old woman squawked and grabbed Kelly by the throat.

"Bad, bad, bad!" she shrieked as she repeatedly hit Kelly in the face with the newspaper. When she finally stopped, the paper was nothing more than a handful of shreds.

"There was a spider in your hair!" Kelly managed, still in shock from the beating Mercy had just given her. The Taser would have been far less humiliating.

Mercy calmed down and the blood drained from her face, restoring it to its naturally pale and waxy complexion.

"A spider?" she asked.

"A big one!" Kelly said. "There it goes!"

She pointed across the room and Mercy looked over. While she was turned away, Kelly took the bobby pin she had managed to yank out of Mercy's hair and tucked into her bra.

Mercy finished up cleaning up the food and stood up.

"I didn't see it," she said. "Maybe I need new glasses."

"Maybe," Kelly replied. "Or you should just try contacts."

"Thank you oh-so-much, doctor," Mercy said, her voice dripping with sarcasm. "I'll keep that in mind."

She started for the door again when she noticed the paisley strip on the floor. She snatched it up and gave Kelly a suspicious look. Kelly held her breath, waiting for Mercy to check the side of her head and realize the bobby pin was missing but she didn't.

"Bed time now," Mercy said. "We'll do the surgery first thing in the morning."

"I really can't do anything to change your mind?" Kelly asked. "You won't let me go so I can get out of here and forget this whole thing ever happened?"

Mercy stared at her thoughtfully, a half-smile forming on her face.

"Of course not," she finally replied. "But I have to admit, of all the pets I've had over the years, you're the only one I've considered putting down."

"Putting down?" Kelly asked.

Mercy's smile stayed on her face as she reached into her tracksuit and pulled out a small snub-nosed revolver.

"I considered doing it tonight as a matter of fact," she said. "But then I figured you just need a little tender loving care."

Kelly stared at the pistol. The old woman had almost killed her. That certainly would have put the kibosh on her escape plan.

"Sweet dreams!" Mercy said in a singsong voice before exiting the room.

She locked the door with an authoritative-sounding "click" and Kelly listened as her footsteps shuffled down the hallway. She reached into her bra and pulled out the bobby pin. She bent it apart and immediately went to work on the padlock that was holding her shackle in place. It was sturdy but it only took a little digging around with the bobby pin for it to click loose. The shackle dropped from Kelly's ankle and she let out a relieved moan that bordered on orgasmic. Kelly quickly clapped her hands to her mouth, hoping it wasn't too loud. She listened for a few seconds but only heard the buzzing of the fluorescent lights hanging from the ceiling. Kelly stood up and stretched, her back letting out a series of satisfying pops and cracks. Once she had the blood flowing again, she went to work on the door. That proved a lot trickier. She dug around in the lock for a few minutes, snapping the first section of the bobby pin in half. Frustrated but not discouraged, Kelly inserted the other section into the lock and moved it around, albeit a little more gently. It was a full fifteen minutes before she finally caught it on something and was able to unlock it. Kelly took a deep breath and turned the knob. It opened and Kelly was free. The hateful and violent urges she had been feeling suddenly evaporated. She was experiencing only joy and a renewed appreciation for life outside this terrible place, regardless of the hardships that awaited her. As she poked her head into the darkened hallway, she realized that no more hardships awaited her. Once her story got out, there would be interviews, articles, a book deal, maybe even a movie. Kelly had always dreamt of the good life and never imagined it actually coming to fruition. At least not like this. Part of her wanted to kiss Mercy to thank her for allowing it to happen. And maybe she would once the old bitch was committed.

As Kelly looked down the hallway, she realized she was probably in the basement and her prison had likely been a pantry at one time. Kelly took one last triumphant look at the room before creeping down the hallway, her bare feet moving soundlessly on the cool tile. She reached the main section of the basement and saw a set of rickety wooden steps leading up to a door covered in chipped white paint. There were some faded brown streaks on it as well. Kelly had the horrible thought that those were bloody fingerprints from past victims but quickly put it out of her head. She needed to stay clear and focused. She wasn't out of the woods yet.

She climbed the stairs as quietly as she could and was almost halfway to the top when one of them creaked. Kelly stopped, half-expecting the door to swing open to reveal an armed and irate Mercy but it remained mercifully closed. Kelly finished climbing the steps and opened the door to find herself in Mercy's kitchen, which was lit by small bulb hanging over the stove. Kelly looked around, hoping to find a back door or a window she could exit through but there was no door and the only windows were above the sink and much too small for her to crawl out of. Once she got out of the kitchen, she figured it was only fifty feet to the front door and then she was home free.

She tiptoed through the kitchen and entered the dining room area. The front door was close now. All she needed to do was keep moving and…

"Do you really think I'm that stupid?"

Kelly froze at the sound of Mercy's voice. A light went on across the room and she found Mercy seated at her dining room table, still clothed in her velour tracksuit.

"Did you really think that nonsense about the spider in my hair fooled me?"

The violent fantasies of murdering the old bitch came flooding back in a hot, angry wave. Kelly didn't want to just kill Mercy; she wanted to rip her to pieces.

"Then why don't you just fucking shoot me and it get over with?" Kelly screamed at her. "Because I'm either leaving here or you're going to have to kill me. If you think I'm going to be some fucking brain-dead pet to you, you've got another thing coming!"

"Oh, but you are," Mercy said. "I told you I'd fix you and I meant it. I just wanted to try something else first. Call it a loyalty test."

"Fuck your loyalty test!" Kelly screamed before making a break for the door. She ran down the hallway and was terrified to see what was waiting for her in front of the door. It was Rick, his head shaved and sporting a large ugly scar that was crudely held in place with black sutures. His expression was blank and a length of drool was hanging from his mouth. He was completely nude save for the bright red collar around his neck with a large metal tag hanging from it. Even from the down the hallway, Kelly could read the name on it. Gingerbread. Of course it was fucking Gingerbread.

"Rick?"

He stared at her without an ounce of recognition in his vacuous eyes. Rick no longer existed. He was Gingerbread now. Kelly dug her heels in and prepared to charge at him.

"Stop her!" came Mercy's booming command but that mattered little to Kelly.

Nothing was going to stop her, not when she was this close. She hit Rick with everything she had but it was like running into a brick wall. She bounced back and fell to the ground. Rick stood over her drooling. He hadn't even flinched and why would he? Mercy had taken great care in ensuring he would not only be a loyal pet but a great watchdog if need be. Kelly started to stand but Rick fell on top of her. He held her in place as Mercy came over with a hypodermic needle at the ready.

"See?" she said, beaming proudly as she injected Kelly with the contents of the needle. "Absolute loyalty. You'll get there, too."

Kelly's final thought before she slipped into unconsciousness was Wyatt's Diner, where this entire fucking clusterfuck had started. It was a bad idea then and a cataclysmic one now. But Kelly had relented to Rick's stupid will, all because she wanted a fucking roast beef sandwich. Fuck that shit.

The food wasn't even that good.

It was a crisp winter morning when Mercy Jerkins awoke to the sound of birds cheerfully chirping outside her window. Christmas had come and gone and it was one of the best ones in recent memory. She hadn't spent it alone and her company had proved more than adequate.

She hummed an old Cole Porter song as she showered and dressed. It was after seven. The pets would need to be walked. She hooked on their leashes and took them outside but not before putting their sweaters on. It was winter after all.

Gingerbread was a good boy who had learned to do his business as soon as they stepped outside. Firecracker was still learning but that was okay. Mercy knew she was going to be a tough nut to crack but she was making progress. And she wasn't without her perks. She had beautiful blonde fur that Mercy loved to style in different braids. She had never had a pet like that before. Sure, she had to shave some of it off for the transformation but there was still more than enough for Mercy to work with.

After they went back inside, she served them their breakfast and Gingerbread ate his ravenously while Firecracker took hers in hesitant, delicate bites. That was okay, too. The first three days after the transformation she hadn't eaten anything, which had worried Mercy some but hunger eventually won out and Firecracker had started to eat. They were still the occasional flashes of anger and even awareness in her eyes but Mercy didn't let that bother her. She knew Firecracker would eventually come around.

Her pets always did.

Clean Slate

"They're ready for you."

The pleasant-sounding voice startled Luke. He had been sitting in the office for over an hour and the soft music they piped in through the ceiling had lulled him slightly, something he cursed himself for. He was a soldier; always trained to be on guard and no doubt the people he was here to see had noticed him dropping his guard.

"Thank you," he said as he stood up and walked briskly toward the non-descript door that sat at the very back of the room. There was a muted buzzing and the door clicked open, allowing Luke to enter.

He headed down a long hallway, trying to make sense of how he had gotten here. A week ago, he had been called into his C.O.'s office and been told five simple words: "They're keen to meet you."

At first, Luke had thought it was a joke. During his basic training days, he had heard talk of an elite unit that superseded all the brass and even the President but he had dismissed it as conspiracy theory nonsense. The rumors continued when he was deployed to Iraq and then Afghanistan. It was said to be a unit that picked the best of the best of the best. You served with them, you were set for life. They'd watch you for a while and then handpick with you those five magical words: "They're keen to meet you.

Luke continued to laugh it off as wishful thinking. When you were in the shit, you'd fantasize about any number of things (mostly girls) but career advancement and wealth also did the trick. Luke reasoned that if such a thing did exist, it wouldn't make much of a difference to him. He was born a soldier (third generation) and would spend his life as one. There had never been any question otherwise. Whether it was sleeping on a cot in some Third World country as a grunt or on a comfortable bed in some D.C. suburb as an officer, Luke was in for life. And he was a good soldier. Highly decorated, well-respected, destined for great things. It was a life well-spent. Mostly, anyway. If he had any regrets, it was that his dedication had caused his one meaningful relationship to break down. His long-time girlfriend Amy had left during his second tour of Afghanistan and was now married and had one kid. Luke didn't hate her or hold any grudges. He knew the lion's share of the blame fell on him. And she had seemingly forgiven him, as they were Facebook friends now (hence knowing about the husband and the kid). Luke accepted her decision but still felt the occasional tugs of sadness and regret. There had been no shortage of women in his life but Amy had been the only one he had truly loved. The only thing he loved more was being a soldier. And apparently that love and dedication had paid off.

Luke reached a cream-colored steel door at the end of the hallway. After a few seconds, another muted buzz let him inside. He opened the door to another waiting room. This one was sparsely decorated with a couch and two chairs that had seen better days. Luke was almost disappointed with how rote everything was. After his C.O. had delivered the message, Luke found a plain white envelope in his mailbox that contained a card with the address of the building printed on it in black ink. The building itself was like any building you'd find in any city. Three stories made of tinted black windows and light brown brick. Luke reasoned it as hiding in plain sight but still, it was a little lame. The teenager inside him had hoped for something ultra-sleek like you'd see in a James Bond film. Crazy gadgets, automated doors that made a "wooshing" sound when they opened. Maybe even a couple of sexy girls in white lab coats. But if all the rumors were true, Luke might be able to buy all of that for himself once this was all over.

"In here, soldier!" a deep voice boomed from the lone office at the front of the room.

Luke walked inside to find the office was not unlike the one his uncle the accountant operated in North Carolina. A man with a large mole on his chin sat at a large desk reading through a folder with a coffee stain on it. Another man, well-built and imposing, stood next to him.

Luke wasn't sure if either of them were brass but, always being the good soldier, stood at attention just to be safe.

"At ease," Muscles said.

Luke did as he was told and waited for them to speak again.

"What do you know about us?" The Mole asked without looking up from the folder.

"Nothing, sir," Luke replied. He had no interest in perpetuating rumors.

"You mean you had never heard of us before now?"

The Mole finally looked up from the folder and stared at Luke with piercing blue eyes. Luke couldn't lie to them. They'd be able to see right through him.

"I've heard rumors going back to basic training," Luke admitted. "But I don't give rumors much credence."

"That's good," The Mole said. "Because I assure you, whatever you've heard is misinformation. There's no way for anyone outside this organization to know what we do. We make sure of it. But we'll explain that later. For now, we just have a few basic questions."

"Of course," Luke said, eager to get down to business.

"You have quite a record," The Mole continued. "Do you like being a soldier?"

"More than anything," Luke answered quickly. "I was born a soldier."

"Good. Because we recruit soldiers. But we deploy operatives. And everything that came before that is going out the window. Do you think you can handle that?"

Luke didn't completely understand but responded in the affirmative.

"Yes, sir."

"One year of service. After that, you'll be given full benefits and a pension that puts you comfortably in the one percent. Most of our ex-operatives settle someplace warm. I recommend Maui."

Although he would likely keep it simple and go to Florida or Arizona, Luke stayed silent and waited for them to continue.

"Your retirement will be permanent. You won't ever hear from us again. Once you do your time, you're home free. How does that sound?"

Luke paused briefly before answering.

"I think that sounds excellent, sir."

"But maybe a little too good to be true?" The Mole asked with a wry smile. "I mean, you'll retire a millionaire? Not even generals can boast that. What's the catch, right?"

Luke had been wondering that but continued to let them do most of the talking. If they were going to save him the trouble of asking the hard questions, he wasn't going to knock it.

"You'll be a ghost," The Mole continued matter-of-factly. "Financial records will be wiped clean, we'll alter your dental and medical records. Your fingerprints will be removed. The process is relatively painless."

"Okay," Luke agreed. Sounded like pretty standard Black Ops stuff. His mother wouldn't be happy but if he explained it would only be a year, she'd more or less accept it. But there had to be more to it than that, right?

And as it turned out, there was.

"We'll be erasing your memory," Muscles said.

It was the first time he had spoken since telling Luke to stand at ease. He said it so bluntly that it took Luke a minute to process it.

"My memory?" he asked.

"What you're going to be doing is stuff the President doesn't even know about. And if he did, he wouldn't want to. To call this work extreme would be an understatement. And while taking you off the grid is an easy enough problem solver, it still doesn't solve all the problems."

"What other problems are there?" Luke asked.

"Your memory," The Mole said, resuming control of the interview. "They'll be able to find out who you are, where you're from, and most importantly, who you work for. And they won't find that info out by waterboarding you and sticking pins in the end of your ding dong.

They don't need to. They can just kill you and extract all the information from your brain."

"Does the technology to do that exist?" Luke mused. It sounded like something out of a Philip K. Dick novel.

"It's existed for some time," The Mole answered. "The only way to ensure complete and absolute confidence is to make sure you're going in with a completely clean slate."

Luke was trying to make sense of this.

"Clean slate?" he asked. "But what about all of my training?"

"Before each assignment, you'll be given the information and training you need through brain implants. So in case you're caught or killed, they won't get any information that they wouldn't have already figured out. And then when you return, we'll wipe you mind clean again and prepare you for your next assignment. Once you've put your year in, you'll get one last memory wipe and spend the rest of your life spending."

They stared at Luke, waiting for him to respond. When he didn't, The Mole leaned forward, his face sympathetic.

"We know it's a lot to ask. That's why the reward is so great. And you're not only doing your country a great service but the world, too. If it weren't for us, the entire planet would have nuked itself years ago."

And while that was significant, Luke wasn't thinking about his service or the reward it would bring. He was thinking about a life where his family and friends would never see him again. Worse yet, a life where he wouldn't even remember any of them.

"He's still unsure," Muscles said. "Tell him the rest."

Luke felt the faintest glimmer of hope. Maybe it wasn't as bad as it sounded.

"We've been watching you for a long time. As such, we know how important your family is to you. If you agree to go forward with this, we'll tell your family you were killed in action and your mother will be given a very generous benefits package. Enough to pay off that house and get rid of that pesky credit card debt. Hell, she invests well and plays her cards right, maybe she can get her own place in Maui. How does that sound?"

"You're going to tell her I died?" Luke asked as he imagined the heartbreak it would cause her.

"For all intents and purposes, you will be dead. At least this way she'll be able to spend her remaining years in comfort."

Luke thought about that. He had his own pension waiting and while it was certainly adequate, it wouldn't clear his mother of her debts or allow her to live in luxury. But still, to never see her again? Or to have her think he's dead? And what about Amy? Sure, she had moved on but he had still been her first love. Luke would certainly be in pain if she died.

"I still don't know," Luke finally replied. "I'm sorry."

"That's fair," The Mole said amiably enough. "Not everybody accepts. And if we part ways today, no hard feelings."

"However," Muscles added. "You've been a good soldier. Exemplary, in fact. And we think such loyalty and service deserve a proper a reward. Don't you?"

"I guess," Luke said. "But you're asking me to sacrifice everything. Literally."

"We understand. But as you told us, you were born a soldier. Don't you want to serve your country in the best possible manner?"

"Sure," Luke replied. "But if there was some other way…"

The two men looked at each other with knowing smiles. This was clearly the moment they were they waiting for.

"We do have something," The Mole said. "Call it a reconditioning program. Three steps. Strictly voluntary."

"It's not mind control, is it?"

They vehemently shook their heads.

"The days of MKUltra are over. We have respect for our operatives. Nothing happens without your consent."

"What are the three steps?" Luke asked, warming to the idea slightly.

"Well, that's the good news," Muscles replied. "You may only need one of them."

"What does it consist of?"

"We won't lie, it's a little rough but if you're serious about this opportunity, it's the only way you'll be able to move forward. Still interested?"

"So this program will what, help me come to terms with essentially losing everyone and everything I hold dear?" Luke asked.

"Something like that. It's a program we've been working on for a while. As of right now, it has a success rate of almost a hundred percent. We're still working on getting it all the way there. And I think we're getting close."

Luke almost blurted out that he didn't believe them, but then stopped himself. A one hundred percent success rate? How would that be possible without some form of mind control?

"Hey, if you don't want to go through with this, fine. But if you've really got the goods, you, your family, and your country will stand to benefit greatly."

Luke felt a cold sweat break out on his forehead. The room suddenly seemed very cramped. He had become a soldier knowing full well the day might come where he'd never see his loved ones again and now that the day had arrived, albeit in a manner he hadn't counted on, was he really going to pussy out when he stood to make a real difference in the world and help his family in the process?

"Fine," he whispered.

"What was that?"

"Fine," Luke repeated, more forcefully this time. "I'm in."

"Good boy," Muscles said with a grin that looked nothing short of vulpine to Luke but it didn't matter.

He had a sinking feeling he had just sealed his fate.

Five minutes later Luke was standing in front of a futuristic door that looked like it would make a "wooshing" sound when it opened. So this stuff did exist. You only got to see it if you were brave (or stupid) enough to move forward with whatever they were about to put him through.

"Enter through here and the reconditioning begins," The Mole said as he scanned a key card in front of the door. True to form, it "wooshed" open.

"When you first step in, you'll see something you need," Muscles said. "Otherwise, we'll be watching. Good luck, soldier."

Luke already hated this. But the guy had just called him soldier.

That was the key. Luke *was* a soldier. One of the best (at least according to them). And he had never been one to shirk his duties. Taking a deep breath, Luke stepped inside and the door closed behind him. The room he had entered was pure white and reminded him of the ending of *2001*. Given how vague and surreal the whole thing had already been, Luke half-expected to see a bed with his much older self in it but the room was empty, save for a podium in the center of the room. Resting on top of the podium was a KA-BAR knife.

Cute, guys, but I'm not a fucking Marine, Luke thought as he carefully picked it up. The blade glinted dully in the harsh fluorescent lighting.

Luke looked up to see a tiny security camera blinked on the ceiling. He stepped below it and held his arms out to express befuddlement at what was expected of him. And in response, there was a "wooshing" sound but it came from the opposite end of the room. A panel on the wall that stood about three feet high had opened up and Luke could hear the faint clicking of claws approaching.

Not knowing what to expect, Luke held the knife in a defensive position and braced himself. The clicking drew closer and something emerged from the opened panel in the wall. And Luke couldn't believe his eyes. It was impossible. It had to be. The thing standing before him was...

"Rex?" Luke croaked.

And his childhood dog, dead four years now, barked in the affirmative.

Rex was adopted into the family when Luke was thirteen. Almost immediately, he and Luke became inseparable. Even Luke's father, who didn't have much time for dogs (or his own children), came to love the dog. And when Luke's father died five years later, Rex had been there for him. A normally energetic dog, Rex sat complacently with Luke, who hadn't cried at the news but still deeply mourned the loss of a man he had never had a proper relationship with. Luke had been overseas when his mother put Rex down at the age of fourteen. Even now, Luke still kept a picture of the dog on his desk. And yet here it was now, staring at him with its long pink tongue hanging out. But it couldn't be Rex. His mother had confirmed the cremation and even spread his ashes over the park they used to take him to. Regardless, this one was a disturbing likeness, down to the canine Rex had chipped when he was three.

"What?" Luke said, as he attempted to put on a brave face for the security camera. "You bring back my dog and that's supposed to make me want to forget my past? Nice try!"

"*Attacke!*"

The retort reverberated through the room at full volume and Rex's doppelgänger came snarling at Luke full-speed, its mouth foaming with thick white saliva. Luke stumbled back and the dog jumped at him, its furry body striking him and knocking him to the ground. It immediately went to work on his arm, causing a deep, steely pain to shoot through it. Luke had the grim realization that his throat would be next. He looked around on the floor and saw the KA-BAR just out of his reach. He gritted his teeth and pulled forward, the gurgling dog still clamped on his arm. Luke was ready to pass out when he finally reached the knife. He grabbed it and with his remaining strength, swung around and planted it firmly in the dog's neck. There was a muffled yelp and its bite relented immediately. The dog dropped to the ground twitching while blood spread over its fur and onto the tiled floor. Still dizzy, Luke took a minute to regain his bearings. He looked at his arm and saw that it now resembled bloody hamburger. Suppressing the urge to vomit, he turned his attention back to the dead dog.

"REX" the bloodied green collar around its neck proudly proclaimed.

And before he passed out, Luke knew with utter certainty it was the real Rex's collar.

Fucking bastards.

When Luke came to, he was still inside the room but his arm had bandaged and there was no sign of the dog.

"How are you feeling?" The Mole asked over the loudspeaker.

"Like I just killed a dog that looked exactly like the one I had as a kid. Nice touch with the collar, by the way."

"Well, we needed the collar to make the clone," Muscles explained. "It had some of the dog's fur on it. You need to do a better job of locking your keepsakes up."

"So that's it?" Luke asked. "You clone my dog, have me kill it, and then I'm okay with my memory being erased?"

"The dog is one of your finest memories, isn't it?" The Mole asked. "Now when you close your eyes and picture it, you'll be planting a knife in his loyal neck."

"That wasn't my dog!" Luke spat at them. "Fuck you!"

"Does that mean you're ready to call it quits? Or do you want to go for the second step?"

"What's step two? Are you going to make me burn down my childhood home?"

"Not exactly," The Mole said. "If you think you can live with killing your childhood dog, then I guess you're ready for step two."

"Yeah, if that's you want," Muscles added. "I mean, you're not going to impress us if that's what you're going for."

Luke stayed silent and determined. He wasn't trying to impress them. If these fuckers wanted to try and torture him by exploiting his memories, they were in for a very rude awakening. Rex had been family.

And *nobody* fucked with his family.

"The next step will begin now. Check the podium again."

Luke stood up and walked over to the podium. Instead of a knife, there was a Sig Sauer waiting for him.

"It only has one bullet, so make it count," The Mole cautioned over the loudspeaker.

For brief and insane second, Luke considered using it on himself but then the door on the opposite side of the room "wooshed" open. A man in fatigues entered pushing a chrome wheelchair. Seated in said chair was a small child who was tied up and blindfolded. He sobbed softly as the man in the fatigues parked the chair and exited the room. As difficult as it was, Luke stared at the kid and decided that he looked vaguely familiar, but was unable to place how he knew him. Maybe it was just leftover paranoia from the ordeal with the Rex clone. Unable to face the child any longer, Luke looked down at the Sig Sauer and a horrible realization fell over him.

"No fucking way!" he said looking up at the camera. "I've done a lot of shit I'm not proud of, but I've never killed a fucking kid! And I won't! Now let me the fuck out of here!"

He walked to the door and pounded it on three times to let them know he meant business.

"Take it easy," The Mole said over the loudspeaker. "You don't have to kill this kid. You have to save him."

The door on the other side of the room "wooshed" opened again and a person wearing a black hood entered, also carrying a Sig Sauer. They took their place next to the child and stood stock-still, facing Luke.

"Remove your mask."

The figure mechanically off peeled the mask and Luke gasped when he saw its face.

Standing before him, dead two years now, was one of his favorite people in the entire world.

His maternal grandmother.

She looked as she did when Luke was a child. She was in her sixties then but still had more energy than people half her age. When he joined the Army, he joked that she'd be able to handle basic training with no problem and would probably even perform better than most of the other recruits. The only blessing with her death was that it had come quickly. A heart attack in her sleep. There had been no real physical or mental deterioration. One day she was there, the next she was gone. As with Rex and his father, Luke was devastated but somehow still managed not to shed any tears over it. He wasn't sure if he believed in Heaven but if it did exist, his grandmother would definitely be there. Him? Not so much. Although it had taken Luke time, he had finally come to terms with the fact he'd never see her again. Like Rex, the thing standing in front of him wasn't a miracle but a perversion designed to corrupt his memories. And he hated himself for agreeing to it.

"Coffee cake."

The two words came over the loudspeaker and while they sounded innocuous, they proved to be anything but. The thing posing as Luke's grandmother raised its own Sig Sauer and pointed it at the back of the child's head. The blindfold made the child mercifully oblivious to this but that wouldn't stop a bullet from passing through his brain. And if the sight of that wasn't cruel enough, coffee cake had been his grandmother's specialty. As far as Luke was concerned, these fuckers were operating on a level of evil that Luke had never encountered before, including the enemies he had been dispatched to fight on three separate occasions.

"You better take her out," The Mole said. "One more command from us and she shoots the kid. And then you. Don't forget you only have one bullet. She's got a whole clip and two to spare. You have until the count of three."

The clone stood its ground, keeping the gun pointed at the kid's head.

"Nana?" Luke asked hesitantly.

The clone didn't acknowledge him. That was enough for Luke.

"One..."

Luke raised the Sig Sauer and fired. The bullet caught the clone in the chest and spun it around before dropping it to the floor. The kid broke into prolonged wails as Luke ran over and kicked the gun away from the clone, who was writhing on the ground as blood poured out of the hole in its chest. Luke stared down at it dispassionately. This wasn't his grandmother, same as the dog hadn't been Rex. And then it spoke.

"Lukey, how could you?" the clone asked, its hazel brimming with tears as blood began to bubble inside its mouth. "It's Nana! I love you!"

"No," Luke uttered, though it was barely audible over the child's screaming.

"They made me do it, Lukey, why didn't you help me?"

"No!" Luke said again, louder this time.

"Why..." it uttered before finally dying, its eyes open and staring up at Luke with a mixture of betrayal and bewilderment.

Luke dropped the gun and fell to his knees. This was an utter fucking nightmare.

"Are you ready? Or do you want to put yourself the third step?" The Mole asked over the loudspeaker.

Luke didn't answer and the child began screaming for his mother.

"Mommy! Mommy!"

"Those clones are something, aren't they?" Muscles asked, seemingly unperturbed by the child's screaming. "We had to use accelerated growth for Nana. We did make a quick stop when she reached her twenties, though. Nana was quite the looker. And quite the lay."

Both of them laughed at this and Luke likened the sound to a death rattle because that's exactly what it was.

They just didn't know it yet.

Luke was guided out of the room a few moments later by two more men in fatigues. Another man in civilian clothing came in and untied the child while doing his best to comfort him. Luke was tempted to ask what was going to happen to the boy but it hardly mattered. Whether he lived or died was out of Luke's hands now. And while Luke felt the deepest sympathy for him, he had his own business to attend to.

"You sure you want to go through with this?" Muscles asked as he handed Luke a bottle of water.

"Clones," Luke said with a shrug before drinking the water down in three huge gulps.

"As long as you know what you're doing," The Mole said as he exchanged an amused glance with Muscles.

Luke did know what he was doing. All too well. And that was extremely bad news for these assholes.

Luke was given another knife before entering the room for the last time. It was almost too perfect. He had been thinking of ways to kill them with his bare hands but a knife was much more ideal. He'd have to go for Muscles first. Once he was dead, taking The Mole down would almost be an afterthought. And just for the hell of it, Luke might even use his bare hands to kill him. But for the moment, he stayed frosty.

He still had to get through the last step.

Luke entered the room a final time to find a person kneeling on the floor with a hood over their head. Their hands were tied behind their back and they were quivering. Luke thought about what abomination might be under there but stopped himself. He'd need what was left of his wits to take these two assholes down.

"Kill the person under the hood and you're good to go."

The Mole's voice had maintained the same detached indifference through this entire hellish process. Luke was nothing to them, just another operative they would exploit and then discard. Luke wondered how much truth there was to the supposed fortune that awaited him when it was all over. Knowing there was no turning back, Luke tightened his grip on the knife and stepped forward, plunging the blade into the person's skull. The body began to spasm underneath the hood. The spasms were so intense that it took a good ten seconds for Luke to pull the blade out. The thing finally collapsed and Luke let out a sigh of relief, playing it up for the camera. He wanted them to think he was exhausted and at ease.

"Sit tight, we're coming in."

Luke gave a brief nod and let the bloodied knife drop to his side.

The door opened and both men entered applauding him. The Mole was even carrying a bottle of champagne.

"Very good," Muscles said. "Not many of operatives make it to the third step. And the majority of them refuse to move forward when they find out what it entails. You're what, one of three people to actually go through with it?"

He looked at The Mole, who nodded in the affirmative.

"Told you the hood was a good idea."

"I still think two clones is one too many," Muscles added. "We've found that the operatives that made it the third step were able to reconcile with the fact that the clones aren't the people or pets they're representing."

"Two clones?" Luke asked. "But there were three steps, right?"

Muscles gave him a weary smile in response.

"Like we told you at the beginning, we're still working on getting the program's success rate to a hundred percent. And I think you helped us figure out how to finally do it."

Luke still didn't understand. Two clones?

"Pull the hood off," The Mole said, uncorking the champagne.

Luke began to feel dizzy again. What had they done? Worse yet, what had *he* done?

Terrified of what he might find but unable to remain in the dark any longer, Luke slowly walked over to the fallen figure. He knelt down and carefully removed the hood, which was already tacky with blood.

Amy.

It was Amy. But a clone of Amy, right? Not...

"Look on the bright side," Muscles said. "At least you saved her kid."

Jesus. The kid. That's why he had looked familiar. The photos on Amy's Facebook page.

"We thought about going with your mother," The Mole explained. "But then we wouldn't have been able to sweeten the pot with the benefits package. So we went with the next best thing. I mean, I know you two had been broken up for a while but I think you'd surprise yourself if you knew how often you checked her social media profiles."

Luke knew exactly how much time he spent checking out her social media profiles. But what could anybody expect? She was the one and he had blown it.

Now faced with the horrible reality of what he had done, Luke did what he had been unable to do for his dog, his father, and his grandmother: He began to cry uncontrollably. He imagined it looked as pitiful and ugly as it felt but he didn't care. And as much as The Mole and Muscles deserved it, he couldn't bring himself to kill them. They had done it. He was reconditioned.

Muscles walked over and put a sympathetic hand on Luke's shoulder.

"Are you ready?"

And amidst his sobbing, Luke told them that he was.

What Slumbers Below

It was a moan. Millie could think of no other word for the strange noise she heard coming from the basement. It was especially alarming considering she and her husband Clyde had lived in that house for seven years without a single incident. Still disoriented from sleep, her first thought was of Kelly. She had tumbled down the stairs and suffered a nasty head injury. Her only means of vocalization were the aforementioned moan. But then sanity set in and Millie remembered that Kelly was an adult woman of thirty living in Chicago with a boyfriend who was a podcaster instead of a doctor or a lawyer.

Her second thought was that the moan had come from Amy, their house sitter. Millie and Clyde didn't travel much but when they did, it was Amy who held the fort. She wasn't the brightest girl but she was sweet and reliable. While Millie didn't exactly think of her as a daughter, she did like Amy a great deal. As such, it would be highly distressing for Millie if anything bad would befall her. Sanity continued to set in and Millie remembered that Amy had left about ten minutes after she and Clyde arrived home from their latest cruise. Millie recalled hearing the labored sound of Amy's rickety Nissan starting before it rumbled unceremoniously down the street. That meant Millie and Clyde were the only ones in the house. And if that were truly the case, who (or what) had made that unsettling sound?

"Clyde," she whispered, shaking her husband awake. She felt her hands sink into the considerable rolls of flesh he had amassed in his golden years. The same rolls his doctors routinely warned him about.

Clyde was unresponsive at first, his buzz-saw snoring continuing unabated.

"Clyde!"

Louder this time and more of a hiss than a whisper.

"Hm?"

The sound was thick and groggy. Waking up Clyde was akin to poking a grizzly bear during hibernation but Millie didn't care. She was not accustomed to strange sounds late at night.

"Someone's in the house," she whispered to him. Silence followed. No snoring and most importantly, no moans.

"What are you talking about?" he asked, sounding more alert.

"I heard a…"

She paused. If she didn't pick the right words, he'd dismiss her and go back to sleep. Par for the course as that was how most of their interactions went these days.

"Someone's creeping around in the basement," she finished.

"You heard someone in the basement?" he asked incredulously.

"Yes," she insisted. "I'm sure of it. I wouldn't have woken you up otherwise."

Clyde sighed heavily in response and pulled the bedspread taut. She had already lost him.

"You couldn't hear a busted jackhammer going to town in a fireworks factory," he finished with a disdainful snort.

That hurt. While it was true Millie's hearing had gone downhill the last few years, she knew what she had heard. Her husband mocking what was becoming a growing handicap was bad enough but the fact he refused to believe her was worse. He was older than her by six years but in his mind, she was the doddering and clueless elderly person that could, at best, be humored but never taken seriously.

She thought of the silent dinners, the nights in front of the television, and the cruises where they buried their faces in their Kindles and never spoke. Most importantly, she thought of the lovemaking that had ceased altogether three years ago. Clyde had been on Viagra but as he continued to gain weight and weaken his heart, his doctor had advised against it. And Clyde was all too happy to dump those little blue pills down the drain.

Millie tried to convince herself that the moan was just the product of her overactive imagination and that her best course of action was to fall back asleep. And she had almost succeeded.

But then she heard it again.

It was unmistakable. Even with her bad hearing and Clyde's snoring, Millie had never been so sure of anything in her life. Somebody was in her basement and they were moaning. Her husband was no help and if she did call the police, she imagined them all laughing at the silly old lady who was hearing things in the middle of the night. No help was coming.

Millie was on her own.

As she crept into the basement, Millie (armed with the pepper spray she kept in her purse) tried to imagine who or what could be making such a strange sound at such a strange time of night. In her younger years, she had been fascinated by the strange and unusual. She spent hours poring over books about UFOs, ghosts, Bigfoot, and the

Loch Ness Monster. She didn't believe any of it but it was delightful to read about just the same.

Once the Internet arrived, Millie found even more resources for the oddities hiding in the crevices of everyday life. Much to Clyde's chagrin, she would spend hours reading about lurid cases like the Amityville murders and the Manson Family. It had only stopped when Clyde waved a massive Internet bill in front of her face. Millie took the hint and moved on to Sudoku. Once that had run its course, she developed a fondness for the silly but addictive games that could be played for free on her smartphone. Had Millie continued her exploration of the weird and unexplained, she likely would have come across what was known as the Stone Tape theory.

Said theory suggests that everyday structures, like walls, roads, and even trees have the ability to absorb energy from emotional or traumatic incidents. Under the right circumstances, these energies could be released or "replayed" for someone in the vicinity of where the original incident took place. It's theorized by some that this is the real cause of haunted houses. What's thought to have been unruly ghosts or spirits with unfinished business is merely just a release of an event long since passed and otherwise forgotten. In the case of the mysterious moan emanating from Millie's basement, it wasn't a replay of one incident.

It was a replay of many.

The moan originated from a room that Clyde and Millie initially used for storage but as Kelly's old bedroom had become Clyde's office, they realized they needed a room for her to stay in. While her visits were infrequent, she still needed a place to sleep. The room in the basement seemed like a reasonable concession, particularly since Kelly enjoyed being on her own. And as her podcaster boyfriend had accompanied her on her last several visits., the basement mercifully spared Clyde and Millie from hearing whatever carnal activities their daughter was currently engaged in. The fact was, Kelly and her boyfriend had a very healthy sex life, particularly when they visited her parents. Such a thought would be perverse and revolting to just about anyone but when it came to that room, healthy sex was a proud tradition.

It began during the house's construction in the late sixties. An amorous worker had brought his girlfriend to the site along with a sleeping bag and a six pack of Iron City beer. They had made love in the only finished room, which happened to the guest bedroom Millie was on her way to investigate. Once the house was finished, a family moved in and the eldest son set up camp in said room. He was a star football player, making him quite popular with the girls at his high school. As such, the room saw a lot of activity, morning and night (though mostly night). After the family moved out, a childless couple became the next occupants. To help break up the doldrums of moving, the pair had impulsively fornicated on the room's cold linoleum floor their first night in the house. Like Clyde and Millie, the couple eventually converted it into a guest bedroom and when they entertained friends from out of town, said friends would develop quite a sexual appetite. One man, a business associate of the husband's, had gone as far to bring back a prostitute in the dead of night. Upon flying home the next day, the man regretted his actions and even felt a little dirty. When the STD tests came back negative, he forgot about it and moved on.

The couple eventually retired to New Mexico and sold the home to Clyde and Millie. By that time their marriage had grown so loveless that the room had no effect on them during the rare times they set foot in it. What kept the room going wasn't just Kelly and her boyfriend but Amy the house sitter. Amy had recently met a nice man at yoga and the two had been spending quite a bit of time together. During her most recent stay at Clyde and Millie's, he had been there just about every night and the sex had been great bordering on incredible. She made a mental note to be available for Clyde and Millie whenever they needed it. It was strange to think that a room in the house of an elderly couple was a catalyst for amazing sex but Amy wasn't one to knock a good thing.

Following the rules of the Stone Tape theory, the room's walls and the floor had absorbed all of this sexual energy (along with some other things that are best left to the imagination). Unable to hold it any longer, the room was releasing it in short bursts and that energy was swirling around the room at a feverish pace.

As Millie entered the basement, the room let out another moan. She stopped and briefly considered running out of the house screaming dressed only in her nightgown and slippers, vowing never to return. But that was silly and exactly the sort of thing Clyde would expect from her. After taking a deep breath, she entered the room with her pepper spray at the ready. She was immediately overwhelmed by a sensation that was both foreign and familiar. She became short of breath as her body quivered helplessly. Something began to bloom in her lower region. At first, it scared her but as she slowly began to understand what it was, she embraced it and prepared for what was to follow.

It didn't take long but every second of it was glorious. Millie felt younger, vibrant, and most importantly, she felt loved. The how and why didn't matter. She took a moment to savor what had just happened. The aftermath left her fatigued but immensely satisfied. It reminded her of the cravings she'd get for cigarettes and cold pizza after the infrequent dalliances she had during her college years.

As she made her way upstairs, she reminded herself that the room had a bed that was almost always unoccupied. Such a notion suddenly seemed criminal to her. She laid down next to Clyde and after listening to him snore and fart for a few moments, she reasoned that spending her nights in that magical room would probably be good for both of them.

But mostly her.

Clyde could go fuck himself.

Cruising

Bobby ducked into the alley, the gunshots ringing in his ears and his partner's blood still warm on his face and hands. As the sirens drew closer, Bobby cursed his avarice and shortsightedness. The job seemed too good to be true but he hadn't walked.

Because stupid him, he needed the money.

A quick glance to his burner phone told Bobby it was 8:32. At that moment, he should have been turning left on Walnut. Bobby was meticulous when it came to the timing of a job and its quickest escape route. Not that any of it meant shit now. The route was blocked and the Tesla Model S that was supposed to be such easy pickings was three blocks away with two flats and a smashed windshield, all thanks to the impulsive actions of the late Rosie Moretti.

Bobby normally worked alone but this time around his bosses had insisted he take along a partner, who turned out to be Rosie. And Rosie just happened to be the nephew of the mafioso who had given Bobby's bosses their start.

Nobody's ever free, he thought miserably as looked around the alley for a way out. The police were seconds away. Bobby's window for escape had closed. Defeated, he raised his arms and prayed they wouldn't shoot him, though the odds of that not happening were nigh existent. He wasn't just a car thief party to an asshole who had opened fire on the police, he was a *black* car thief party to an asshole who had opened fire on the police. He might as well have a worn a bullseye. It was only after the alley began to fill with blue and red lights that he noticed the car.

It was strange he had only discovered it just now, especially given its size. The lean, sleek body was roughly the size of a speedboat and the entire thing had been painted a black so shiny it looked almost liquid. Unable to make sense of this anomaly, Bobby blinked and the car was gone. A mere hallucination of what should have been. Or maybe he was just losing his mind. At that moment, the latter explanation was the only thing that made sense. But when he blinked again, the car was back.

And its driver side door was wide open and waiting for him.

The first thing Bobby noticed was the odor. He could smell it faintly outside the car but once he got inside, it completely enveloped him. It was a vile concoction of rancid meat, B.O., and a sour stench that invoked the sensation of bile belching up his throat. His first instinct was to run and not get any vomit on the smooth leather interior but time was up. Police cars were pouring into the alley like a line of frenzied ants.

Bobby had stolen his share of cars, most of them luxury, but he had no clue what the fuck he was looking at. There was no sign of an ignition switch, just a series of strange buttons and dials that littered the dashboard. Even if one of them acted as a starter, he wouldn't know where to begin. Mercifully, the car growled to life and lurched forward. One side of the alley was filled with police cars while the other had a lone warrior parked at the very end. He stood outside his car with a shotgun perched on his hip.

Bobby took a deep breath and placed his hands on the steering wheel before quickly jerking them back. It was ice cold. He tucked his hands into his sleeves and put them back on the steering wheel. Even through the thick cotton of his hoodie, Bobby could feel the stiff cold of the chrome on his skin. He slammed his foot on a pedal that was almost comically oversized and the car began bearing down on the single cop car at the end of the alley. Although there was no speedometer, Bobby figured the car to be doing seventy and it had done that in less than two seconds.

The cop did a nervous shimmy as the car bore down on him. He managed to squeeze off one shot but the barrel was pointed nowhere near Bobby. He dove to safety just as Bobby's car ripped through the cruiser like it was an empty beer can.

Bobby whooped with equal parts joy and relief as the car flew down the street with a bevy of police cars struggling to keep up.

"My own personal Batmobile!" Bobby bellowed happily. What other explanation was there? Some rich jackass in the midst of a midlife crisis had decked out an old sedan with every bizarre bell and whistle imaginable. It wasn't without its flaws of course (the odor being the worst) but it was still saving Bobby's ass. Freedom suddenly seemed like a very real possibility.

And then his phone buzzed.

The sensation was jarring at first. He kept the phone in his hip pocket and while a vibrating phone wasn't unusual most of the time, his present circumstances dictated a much different reaction. First off, it was a burner phone. Other than his employers, nobody had the number. And the rules with the burner phone were firm: Calls went out, not in, and only in the event of the direst emergency. Irrational thoughts began clouding Bobby's brain – the police had gotten a hold of the number and were calling to negotiate. Or better yet, it was his mother. Six years dead and still disappointed with her luckless son. As absurd as both those notions were, they didn't hold a candle to who (or what) was really behind the call.

"Hello?"

Bobby was cruising along at what had to be ninety miles an hour and there was no sign of the police anywhere. After everything that had happened, why not answer the phone? It was an action he would immediately regret. He repeated his greeting but the only response was a low hissing sound. He could almost feel the hot, moist air blowing into his ear. Just as he was about to hang up. a voice came on.

"I believe you have my car."

The words were simple but their speaker gave them a cadence that was refined and elegant.

"Come again?"

"My car," the voice answered calmly. "You have taken what's not yours and I would like it back."

He maintained his elegant cadence but it had grown slightly disquieting.

"I didn't take it," Bobby stammered. "It invited me."

As ridiculous as that sounded, it was true. But the mysterious caller wasn't having it.

"Yes," the voice sighed. "It does have something of a mind of its own. Drawn to bad people, I'm afraid."

That stung. Who the fuck was this guy? Bobby wasn't bad. He had just fallen on hard times. At least that's what he told himself.

"Look, man," Bobby said, trying to sound firm. "This hasn't been a good night. I get safe, I'll ditch your car. I'll even tell you where you can find it."

"Not good enough, my young friend. Pull over now or you'll force me to resort to rather unfortunate measures."

There were still no police cars in sight but that hardly mattered. Haven existed but it was miles in the opposite direction. Ditching the car now would be suicide. The caller's words were chilling but what could he really do? Getting the number to Bobby's burner phone was an impressive and somewhat unsettling feat but beyond that, Bobby was still calling the shots.

"Sorry, man," he finally said. "I need it. And probably a hell of lot more than you do."

"That is regrettable," the voice replied. "But if I were you right now, I'd pay mind to the three police cars up ahead."

Three police cars? What the hell was this guy talking about? The road was almost completely clear. Just as Bobby was set to tell his new friend what was what, the aforementioned police cars zoomed onto the road from a side street, with one of them nearly T-boning him.

"Jesus!" he screamed as hot blood began pounding in his temple. If that wasn't bad enough, the voice on the phone was laughing.

"Oh, I think he'll be steering clear of this mess," the voice chuckled. "And can you blame him?"

Bobby couldn't. And the police cars, all Dodge Chargers, were nipping at his heels.

"My young friend, my patience has run out. Pull over now."

Bobby looked at the spasming red and blue lights and shook his head.

"No fucking way. If I wasn't going to pull over before, I'm sure as shit not going to do it now!"

"Would you like to make the cops go away?" the voice purred seductively in his ear.

"Yes," Bobby said in a flat monotone. The voice, unsettling though it was, had a hypnotic quality.

"Then you'll want to hit the brakes," the voice instructed. "Right about…now."

And without thinking, Bobby brought his foot down on the oversized pedal. The large vehicle immediately came to a silent halt. No screeching tires, no shifting cargo. The next sound Bobby heard was the shrieking crunch of metal as one of the Chargers slammed into the rear of his mysterious getaway vehicle. An explosion followed but Bobby felt no force or heat, both of which were great enough to drive one Charger into the median and the other into a minivan that had the misfortune of being in the wrong place at the wrong time.

A minivan, Bobby thought as hot tears stung his eyes. He prayed there were no kids inside.

"Problem solved!" the voice announced triumphantly. "Now you can return what's rightfully mine."

Bobby turned around and saw the road was a mess of flaming debris and twisted metal. There was no way the cop inside survived. And who knew about the other two cars?

"Drive," the voice commanded, its tone seductive again.

And that's what Bobby did.

But not without reservations.

"What the fuck is this thing?" he asked a few miles down the road, unable to keep his voice from quavering.

"In the most basic sense, it's a vehicle," the voice replied. "Stripped to its essence? Well, that's a bit more complicated and there's certainly no time to explain. Now will you be pulling over or will I be resorting to those unfortunate measures I was hoping to avoid?"

"If you're able to do shit to me when I'm going ninety miles an hour, why do you need a car in the first place?" Bobby asked. He could feel his confidence slowly coming back.

"I have a rather unique connection with this vessel," the voice explained. "You could say wherever it goes, I go."

With a paranoid jolt, Bobby turned around and checked the backseat. It was empty.

"You can relax," the voice assured him. "I'm not in the car. Not yet, anyway. As for why I need it, well, the sprawled-out nature of your country rather requires it, yes? And it's not like I can just turn into a bat and fly away."

The voice then chuckled in a manner that reminded Bobby of dry leaves rasping against a rusted screen.

"Will you be pulling over?" the voice followed up in a more measured tone.

Bobby didn't need to think about his answer.

"No," he said. "Because in case you aren't up on current events, there's a dead cop a few miles back."

An agonizing pause followed. Just as Bobby wondered if the call had been disconnected, the voice replied with three simple words:

"Very well then."

The line went dead and Bobby was immediately overwhelmed by a putrid smelling heat. Within seconds, it had become unbearable, leaving Bobby no choice.

He had to pull over.

Bobby pulled into a side street and parked in front of a building that had once been a bakery. He opened the door and fell onto the mercifully cool pavement. Bobby lay against it until his body cooled down and his nausea subsided. He sat up and listened for the sirens. They were faint but still fast approaching. He looked at the car and reasoned that it had outlived its usefulness, anyway. It was far too conspicuous and now that he was no longer cornered in an alley, he might stand a fighting chance of getting away. He started to run when he heard the unmistakable click of a hard-soled heel nearby. Not one to tempt fate any further, he started to run faster but the clicking only increased. The mysterious footsteps were now almost perfectly in step with his. With the sirens getting even closer, Bobby couldn't afford to be slowed down.

"Hey, what the fuck—" he began, spinning around, only to feel an icy, claw-like hand grip his throat.

Bobby gasped and choked as he was slowly raised up, his feet dangling uselessly over the pavement.

"I tried to warn you," a familiar voice hissed, its breath even more rancid than the inside of its car.

Bobby tried to get a look at his assailant but it kept itself concealed in the shadows. He reasoned that was probably a good thing.

"Under ordinary circumstances, I'd split you from groin to head," the voice continued. "But this is a rather unique situation. Just listen."

Bobby did. He could only hear the sirens that were growing closer by the second.

"They think you killed one of their own," it hissed. "Between that and the color of your skin, I suspect they'll be more than happy to do my dirty work for me."

It laughed again, making the same chilling dead leaves against rust sound it had made over the phone.

"Good luck, my friend."

It dropped him on the ground just as the police cars began to turn the corner. The strange car and its owner had disappeared, leaving Bobby alone with a fleet of angry cops. As they bore down on him with their guns drawn, he knew all too well that his new friend's prediction would prove correct. In his final moments, a familiar thought invaded Bobby's terrified brain:

Nobody's ever free.

Goddamn fucking right.

Drained

It was Saturday night when the attacks on Jerry's farm began. It was after midnight and he could hear the agitated mooing of his cows. His first thought was that the coyotes had come back but that didn't really concern him. It's not like they had the ability to take any of the cows away. Still, stressed-out cows could mean bad milk or lowered productivity and Jerry definitely didn't want to deal with that. He grabbed his shotgun and went outside.

All of his farmhands had gone home hours ago, leaving Jerry alone to fend for himself and his property. And that suited him just fine. What good was a man if he couldn't defend his home and by extension his business and livelihood? While his farm wasn't the biggest in California (he owned just under one hundred cows), he still managed to serve most of the state and a good chunk of southern Arizona with his products. He lived well but not extravagantly, which meant he had already exceeded his own expectations. His father had worked as a janitor in a mental hospital. He had scrimped and saved his entire life and had jack shit to show for it when he died of a heart attack at fifty-eight. So not only had Jerry exceeded his father's income by a considerable margin, he had already outlived him by six years.

The cows continued their panicked chorus of mooing and baying, leaving Jerry to wonder if some shithead kids had wandered on to his farm and were harassing them. It wasn't a common occurrence but it did happen on occasion. Jerry had fired a couple of shots at the last group of little assholes that had made that mistake and one set of parents had actually come to his farm the next day and threatened to sue him. Jerry politely informed them that they'd have to account for trespassing, destruction of private property, and cruelty to animals if they went that route. The couple had then shrieked to the heavens that they were still going to sue him and see to it that all the local grocery stores boycotted his products but Jerry had never heard another word about it. There hadn't been any trespassers since and Jerry was rather proud of himself for that. He could only assume if there were intruders on his farm, they were new to the area and hadn't learn he was somebody you didn't fuck with.

Jerry entered the barn and found several of the cows banging around in their stalls, almost as if they were trying to escape. That wasn't a good sign. Cows were about the laziest and most docile creatures he had ever come across, so if they were this spooked, something was definitely wrong. When Jerry reached the middle of the barn, he saw why. Two of his cows lay dead with their necks broken. Their vacant eyes stared up at the ceiling and their oversized pink tongues were hanging out their mouths and touching the sawdust-strewn ground.

Jerry raised the gun and looked around, the remaining cows still mooing and bashing their thick bodies against the side of their stalls. Nothing else was out of the ordinary so Jerry set his gun down and did his best to calm the agitated cows down by stroking their heads and giving them some extra food. Once they were relaxed, he examined the two dead ones. He had never seen anything like it. The amount of strength it would take to snap their necks would be immense. And as he looked closer, he discovered something even more unsettling. Both cows had two small holes at the base of their throats. A little bit of blood had clotted around the holes but otherwise the wounds were almost indiscernible. What could have done something like this?

Jerry was startled from this disturbing thought by something crashing to the ground nearby. He jumped to his feet with his shotgun ready as the cows resumed their perturbed baying.

"Whoever you are, show yourself!" Jerry called out. He crept toward the back of the barn with the shotgun raised but found it empty. It was just him and the cows.

Unable to do anything else tonight without his farmhands, Jerry spat on the ground and went back inside. Dawn was just a few hours off and he was in for a long day.

The morning arrived and after Jerry finished the morning chores, he called Bill Carson over to take a look at the dead cows. Bill was Jerry's usual vet and a decent enough guy. And he'd be willing to keep his mouth shut (provided Jerry threw him a little extra scratch).

"Goddamn!" Bill said, kneeling down next to the dead cows, which were already attracting flies (more than usual anyway). Jerry had his farmhands drag the cows out of the barn. They were a little taken aback with the state of them but Jerry had barked at them to keep quiet about it. That cost of that would be a case a beer and an extra hundred bucks at the end of the week. Mysterious deaths were proving to be a costly venture.

"Have you ever seen anything like it?" Jerry asked him, knowing full well what Bill's answer was going to be.

"Nope. The broken necks are strange enough. I've seen some

animals crash into the sides of houses and buildings and break their necks that way but that's not the case here. Their heads have been twisted almost clean off."

"What about the holes?"

Bill ran his gloved finger over one of them before sticking his finger inside it. It made a squishing sound that almost caused Jerry to puke up the bacon and eggs he had eaten for breakfast.

"They're definitely bites of some kind," Bill said, twisting his finger around in the hole. "But I'll be damned if I know what did it."

He removed his finger and Jerry was sickened to see it wasn't covered in blood but some kind of clear fluid.

"What the hell is that?" Jerry asked, pointing at it with a long, shaking finger. "There's no blood."

Bill stared at his gloved hand in disbelief before carefully peeling it off and placing it in a baggie he produced from his pocket.

"If it's all the same to you, I'd like to test it and do an autopsy on the animal," he said. "Can your boys bring it to my office later?"

Jerry hesitated. Bill was a good man but Jerry didn't like the idea of the cow leaving the farm when they still weren't sure what caused it. Jerry enjoyed a successful business that didn't draw much attention. He wanted to keep it that way. The thought of his farm showing up on that goddamn YouTube gave him even more distress than the dead cows. Bill seemed to pick up on this.

"Have them bring it to the back of my office tonight," he said. "No one will be the wiser."

"Thanks," Jerry said but even that didn't put him totally at ease. Something was seriously wrong here.

And Jerry, being a man of routine and control, didn't like that one bit.

Evening came and Jerry was seated in his kitchen eating a dinner of steak and braised potatoes. The beef was supposedly prime cut but it tasted like shoe leather to Jerry. The dead cows were gone, currently being transported on the interstate by two of his farmhands. He had given them money for dinner and a promise of an extra two hundred bucks at the end of the week. Jerry didn't know what Bill would find but his biggest fear was that his cows had contracted some kind of strange disease when they were attacked, which would mean all sorts of attention. And farms that were revealed to be ground zero for some unknown disease didn't tend to last very long.

Jerry helped himself to some Jack Daniels after dinner and then went outside to check the barn. The cows seemed complacent; some of them had even fallen asleep. As Jerry scanned the stalls filled with stupid creatures almost completely devoid of personality, he was a little saddened to realize they were the closest thing to a family (or friends) he had. His wife Nancy had left him ten years ago and he hadn't spoken to his son Andy since then. And as far as Jerry could tell, it was Nancy who had poisoned Andy against him. His only son and she had the fucking gall to take him away, too.

"I guess ruining our marriage wasn't enough for you!" Jerry slurred to the dull and bored-looking cows.

This was the downside of drinking Jack. Sometimes it could serve to put Jerry's nerves at ease but mostly it just brought a lot of bad memories to the surface. They were easy enough to repress when he was working on the farm, which didn't allow downtime. That was the main reason Jerry liked it. Owning a farm meant purpose, repetition, and best of all, distraction. Jerry was about to go inside and pour himself another glass of Jack when he heard something moving around in the grass outside the barn. Several of the cows stirred and began to shift around in their stalls.

Jerry pulled a small flashlight out of his pocket and walked outside the barn to see who (or what) decided to pay him an unexpected visit. He pointed the flashlight around but saw only the tranquil twilight of another perfect California night. The long grass swayed and whispered in the calm breeze. It reminded Jerry of that film *Days of Heaven*. He had taken Nancy to see it on their second date and…

Jerry halted the memory and did his best to push it out his head. Fucking Jack Daniels.

He continued to survey the area but the coast was clear. He wondered if a rabbit or a stray cat he decided to cut through his property. Either way, whatever it was had moved on. Jerry took a step forward and felt his left foot squish into a patch of cold, slimy mud. Jerry mumbled a string of profanities and pointed his flashlight at the ground. His foot had left a messy imprint in the reddish-brown mud but what sat to its immediate right almost caused Jerry to scream.

It was a shallow footprint with three razor-clawed toes.

Something had been here. And it definitely wasn't human or any animal Jerry had ever seen before.

He suddenly understood that his problems were just beginning.

Jerry took several pictures of the footprint and made a cast of it with some Plaster of Paris he had in the garage. He wasn't sure about leaving the cows alone, so he called one of his farmhands and offered him three hundred to stay outside for the evening. The farmhand had accepted and showed up twenty minutes later, his eyes slightly bloodshot. Jerry guessed he had been drinking or smoking pot but it seemed like as long as there was a human around, the animal likely wouldn't attack. Just the same, Jerry made a note not to ask this particular farmhand for something like this again (especially if it was going to cost him three hundred bucks a pop).

Jerry helped himself to a little more Jack Daniels before going to bed. Usually it was the perfect sleep aid but he was restless for almost the entire night. The only comfort was that he didn't hear a gunshot. When sleep finally did come, Jerry had mostly sobered up but was sporting a bad headache.

The day hadn't even begun yet but Jerry was already dreading it.

When he woke up, he saw it was nine o'clock. He had overslept by four hours. He got out of bed, his head throbbing like a decaying tooth. When he went outside, his farmhands were already busy with the morning routine. Burnouts or not, they at least attempted to be dependable.

"Hey, boss!" one of the called out. "Ray left a couple of hours ago, said they were no problems."

Jerry nodded at him and went back inside. As he put a pot of coffee on, his phone rang. He checked the display and saw it was Bill.

"Good morning," he answered, knowing full well it was anything but.

"Morning, Jerry," Bill said. "Any problems last night?"

"No, I had one of my workers sit outside," Jerry replied. "No issues."

"Glad to hear it," Bill said before trailing off into a pregnant pause.

Shit. This was going to be bad.

"Did you do the autopsy?" Jerry asked, dreading Bill's answer.

"I did."

"And?"

There was another pause.

"Come on, Bill," Jerry said, annoyed. "You tell little Suzie every day that her favorite pet is going to doggy heaven. You can't be straight with me?"

"Well, that's the thing," Bill said. "I can wrap my head around doggy heaven. I can't wrap my head around this."

"What do you mean?"

"Those teeth marks don't belong to any animal that's officially been documented," Bill answered. "And there's traces of saliva. I can send it out to get tested..."

"No, don't do that just yet!" Jerry interrupted. "Are you at your office?"

"Yeah, but I've got appointments until six."

"Can I meet you there? I found something last night. Maybe it'll help identify whatever that thing is."

"I guess," Bill said, already sounding a little tired.

"Dinner and a hundred bucks if you do," Jerry offered.

"Jerry, I'm happy to take your money but if this is a new species of some kind, we can't sit on this for too long," Bill replied.

"I understand. I'll see you at six."

Jerry hung up and sat down at the kitchen table.

A new species. Maybe something like that would actually be good for business. Assuming they didn't spend months testing it and his herd to make sure it wasn't going to spread something hazardous. There was no way Jerry's farm could survive for that long.

And by extension, neither could he.

When he arrived at the squat redbrick office that housed Bill's office, he noticed that Bill's sporty little Fiat was the only vehicle in the small parking lot. He had likely sent the rest of his staff home, which was a relief for Jerry. Not just because he didn't want anybody else knowing his business but because he wanted to avoid the bullshit small talk Bill's receptionist always insisted on having with him.

He walked in with the plaster cast of the footprint wrapped carefully in a blanket and saw the office was almost completely dark.

"Bill?" Jerry called out.

"Back here," Bill answered from one of the examination rooms.

Jerry worked his way through the darkened waiting room, silently cursing Bill. Couldn't he leave a fucking light on?

He stepped into the examination room and saw Bill seated at a laptop.

"Good evening," Bill said, sounding chipper despite the bags under his eyes.

"Howdy," Jerry said, pulling a stack of twenties out of his pocket and handing it to Bill. Business first.

Bill pocketed the cash without a word and motioned for Jerry to sit down next to him.

"So what do you have for me?"

Bill unwrapped the blanket and brought out the plaster cast. Bill examined it and then smirked.

"Are you sure somebody isn't putting you on?"

"What do you mean?"

"Well, it's an awfully shallow footprint. I have a hard time believing a creature this small could do such a number on an animal as large as a cow."

"Do you really think this is a coincidence?" Jerry asked, frustrated with Bill's dismissive and cavalier response. "Two of my herd get killed by a creature you can't identify and then the next night I find this on my property?"

"I honestly don't know, Jerry," Bill said. "But I'd expect the creature that killed your cows to be a hell of lot bigger than this. Based on the size of the footprint and the depth of the impression, this thing can't be more than three feet tall and probably only weighs about eighty pounds."

"Well, if you don't what the hell it is, how do you know it's not strong enough to do something like that?"

"That's a good question. Let's see what we can find on the Internet."

Bill turned to his computer and started typing. Jerry watched as scanned a number of nature sites but outside of the usual (bears, bobcats, deer), nothing turned up.

"Hang on, I have an idea. Don't think I'm too crazy when I show you this."

Bill typed something into the search engine and Jerry rolled his eyes. It wasn't just crazy. It was stupid. Bill had gone to a cryptozoology site. Bigfoot, The Loch Ness Monster, all things only crazy people believed in. And Jerry wasn't crazy. Not yet, anyway.

Bill continued to scan the site before stopping on an image.

"Well, looks we've got a match."

He turned the screen so Jerry could get a closer look. When he saw what it said, he didn't know whether to laugh or smash Bill's laptop to pieces in a blind rage.

The caption below the footprint (which looked exactly the one found on Jerry's farm) had only one word:

Chupacabra.

"Are you fucking kidding me?" Jerry asked Bill. They spent the next half an hour looking at illustrations of the creature. The only "real" photo was a coyote with a bad case of mange.

"If that thing were fucking real, how do you explain breaking their necks? I shit bigger than that little bastard!"

"Well, ants are known to carry up to five thousand times their body weight," Bill suggested with a grin.

"I've seen ants. You've seen ants. The little buggers invade my kitchen every summer. I've never seen one of these and neither have you. You know why? Because they don't exist!"

"Relax, Jerry!" Bill said, motioning for him to calm down.

Relax? Jerry wanted to smash Bill's laptop over his bald ass head!

"I don't think this creature exists. I still think the footprint is just somebody putting you on. Poor timing, I know..."

"No, it's not poor," Jerry interrupted. "It's perfect. Two of my cows end up dead and then somebody decides to prank me a day later when I kept the whole thing secret? That's no coincidence."

"Well, who knows besides me?" Bill asked. "Your farmhands?"

"They know to keep their mouths shut and they certainly know not to play stupid pranks," Jerry responded pointedly. And they did. Two years back a few of them had the bright idea of putting grease on the door handle of his newly restored '68 Mustang. Jerry had raised such a hell that one of the men actually left in tears and he had fired the rest. That had earned him a reputation and the subsequent help he attracted were desperate men that couldn't find employment anywhere else. They wouldn't risk burning their bridges with him. Which left only Bill.

"It wasn't me, Jerry," Bill said, putting his hands up defensively. "And I haven't said a word, not even to Agnes."

Agnes was Bill's wife and just about the biggest gossip in town. If she knew, so did the entire town. With that in mind, Jerry guessed it would have invoked a much bigger response than some joker leaving fake footprints around his property. All this shit was starting to take its toll on Jerry. He suddenly felt very old and very tired.

"I'm going home," he said weakly. "When do you think you'll get results on that saliva?"

"Could be two days, could be two weeks," Bill replied. "Depends on how backed up they are."

"Well, if you need to grease the wheels a little bit, let me know," Jerry said. "I'm willing to pay."

And although it was true, he privately cringed when he said it. This incident was growing more complicated and expensive with each passing day. He couldn't wait to see what tomorrow brought.

When Jerry got home, he made sure the farmhand who was standing guard had enough to eat and drink. He said he did, so Jerry went to bed. He skipped the whiskey that night, which was good, as the bottle was almost empty. And that stuff wasn't cheap. Based on how the last few days had gone, Jerry wasn't expecting to be able to buy another bottle anytime soon, so it was probably best to make this one last.

Despite how tired he felt at Bill's office, Jerry struggled to fall asleep that night. The idea that something was attacking his business was deeply troubling. Jerry knew he was a hard and even unlikable man but it had served him well. He ran a successful farm that he had built from scratch with shrewd and steady hand. And even if it had cost him his family, he certainly didn't set out to make trouble for others. So why had the universe suddenly turned against him?

The bitterness he felt at this injustice collected like bile in his stomach and throat but it also proved to be a strangely effective sleep aid. Just as he was about to drift off, he heard a gunshot.

Followed closely a scream.

Jerry ran outside with his shotgun at the ready. The cows were going crazy again. He had an ugly vision where his entire herd was dead, their bloated, bloody bodies strewn around the barn Jerry had taken out a bank loan to build (a loan he had paid back in just under ten years). When he reached the barn, the cows were badly shaken but still alive. Jerry called for his farmhand, who didn't respond. Christ, was he dead? Dead cows were bad enough but Jerry didn't even want to imagine the kind of heat he'd get for having a dead person on his property.

"Over here, boss!" came the strained and terrified reply. Jerry pointed the shotgun and walked slowly toward the farmhand's voice. He found the man cowering behind one of the pasteurizing machines.

"What the hell?" Jerry hollered at him.

"I'm sorry, boss, but I ain't never seen anything like that!" the man exclaimed, his eyes wet and his face ashen.

"You've never seen anything like what?" Jerry challenged.

The man shook and his breath came in short gasps before he finally responded.

"Some kind of fucking lizard. 'Cept it was walking upright!"

Jerry couldn't believe it.

"Some kind of fucking lizard? Let me guess? Three feet tall with claws?"

"This thing wasn't no three feet tall!" the man insisted. "It was bigger than me!"

Jerry tightened his grip on the shotgun.

Who the fuck did these people think they were?

Jerry had sent the man packing shortly after that. Well, that wasn't *totally* accurate. The man had thanked Jerry but said he didn't think he'd be coming around anymore. In fact, he told Jerry he was probably going to move to New Mexico and live with his uncle. And that was fine with Jerry. However, not wanting any bad feelings, Jerry pressed an extra three hundred bucks into the man's palm and asked for his silence. The man had agreed, telling Jerry even if he wanted to tell somebody, who would believe him?

After the man had left, Jerry brought a lawn chair and his bottle of Jack outside to keep an eye on his herd. He guzzled the remainder of the bottle in less than thirty seconds, his throat burning like he had swallowed hot sand.

He didn't know when he exactly passed out but when he woke up the next morning with a stiff neck and an even stiffer back, he found three more of his herd dead.

As he stared at the dead and pathetic-looking cows, Jerry wished he were anything but a fucking dairy farmer. He thought back to his father the janitor; a man who had to clean up shit, piss, and jizz on a daily basis. Jerry had vowed never to subject himself to work that demeaning. When Jerry was growing up, his father had seemed so stupid and simple but now Jerry was starting to think the man was a genius. He certainly never had to contend with something like this.

Who the fuck did?

Despite his nasty hangover, Jerry was already digging the graves for the dead cows when his farmhands showed up. Today the milk went out for delivery. Nothing could look amiss.

"Grab a shovel!" he barked at his farmhands as sour-smelling sweat dripped from his head and body.

They stared at the dead cows before turning to Jerry.

"You know, maybe it's time to call the police or animal control or something," one of them suggested.

"And get shut down? Can't afford it!" Jerry said, his aging joints shrieking with pain as he continued to lift shovelfuls of dirt from the ground.

His farmhands obediently grabbed shovels and helped Jerry dig. Within an hour, they had a hole deep enough to drop all three cows in and give them enough time to prepare for the trucks that were set to arrive after lunch.

Jerry and the men worked hard and the trucks were loaded up three hours later without a hitch. Jerry gave the men money for lunch and then went inside his house and collapsed on his bed. He was getting too old for this shit. He decided not to drink that night and pay two of his men to stay and keep watch. More than anything, he wanted to talk to his wife and son. His marriage with Nancy had ended so bitterly that there were scars that would never heal and while Jerry wanted to see his son, he knew facing the now-grown man who hated him would be even more painful than seeing Nancy again.

Still, Jerry found himself staring at his phone.

Was it really too late?

Bill called an hour later and interrupted Jerry from what was a very satisfying nap. Although he unleashed a string of profanity a mile long when his phone went off, he was eager to hear what Bill had to say. Hopefully he had an answer that wasn't a made-up creature.

"Give me good news, Bill!" he said, skipping the formalities.

"I'll try, but what's your definition of good news?" Bill replied.

"News that's better than finding three more of my herd dead?"

"Really?" Bill asked. "Did they die the same as the others?"

"They did."

"And did you…"

"They're buried, Bill," Jerry answered. "I had trucks coming today. Having them pull up and see dead cows is not how I wanted my products to go out this week."

"Fair enough," Bill said. He paused, which drove Jerry nuts.

"So why are you calling?" he finally asked Bill.

"Tests came back from the lap," Bill said. "The good news is that there aren't any strange bacteria or toxins. The bad news is that bite marks come from something in the Reptilia class that hasn't been identified yet."

"So some kind of lizard?" Jerry asked, picturing the illustration of the bi-pedal Chupacabra they had found on Bill's computer. He didn't bother to mention his farmhand's meltdown from the night before.

"Could be," Bill answered. "But that's not to say I think it's the thing we found on the Internet."

"No shit?"

"It's possible it could be some animal that wandered in from the desert," Bill suggested.

"Let's hope. I've got two of my guys staying over tonight to keep watch," Jerry said.

"Are you sure you don't want to bring somebody in on this?" Bill asked. "I know some guys who would be discreet."

"No," Jerry replied before hanging up without a proper goodbye. This was already out of hand but inspiration struck and Jerry went outside. His farmhands were all busy but dropped what they were doing when they saw him.

"I'm no longer asking you to stand guard. I'm asking you to go on a hunt," he announced.

"What do you mean, boss?" one of them asked.

"A hundred dollar a week a raise and a thousand-dollar bonus to the man who kills the thing that's attacking the farm," Jerry replied. "Any takers?"

The men looked impressed. Jerry had his huckleberries.

Jerry fixed himself a cup of tea and looked outside at the men, who were seated in lawn chairs and flipping through their phones with their shotguns propped up next to them. They had already done a lap around the property but didn't find anything. Jerry suggested they take a break and do another lap of the property after midnight. He didn't like them having their guard down but at least they weren't drunk and on the verge of passing out. Jerry secretly cursed himself for being guilty of that.

He knew the men both had girlfriends and were likely texting with them. He had asked for their discretion and had likely gotten it but he still couldn't help but feel a little envious. The farm had become his whole life and he hadn't realized just how dangerous that was. You always needed something to fall back on if your life went to shit. And Jerry didn't have anything else. If his farm went under, Jerry would be doomed to living in his sister's basement or worse.

Acting on pure impulse (something he hadn't done since high school), Jerry took out his phone and dialed Nancy. There were several rings and Jerry began to wonder if she still had the same number until her voice, which had always sounded like music to Jerry, came alive on the other end.

"Hello?"

"Nancy?" Jerry croaked.

There was a pause followed by a weary sigh.

"What do you want, Jerry?"

"You don't sound happy to hear from me," he said, hoping she could detect the attempt at good humor in his voice.

"And you didn't answer my question. What do you want?"

Jerry gritted his teeth. This was already going poorly and they had barely made it past hello.

"I don't know," he finally responded. "Guess I just needed a familiar voice to talk to."

Silence again but Jerry could actually feel her soften over the distant and crackling connection. Being open about his feelings was not one of Jerry's strong suits; it had actually been one of the many things that had ended their marriage.

"What's wrong?" she asked, her voice slightly huskier with age but still just as beautiful as they day they had met.

"You name it," Jerry replied. "In addition to Murphy making sure his law is working against me nonstop, he's taken to spreading his cheeks and blasting me with as much shit as he can squirt out. The clean-up's getting a bit tedious."

"I can imagine," Nancy replied with a dry chuckle. "You always had an interesting way with words, Jerry."

"And did it without ever reading a book," Jerry announced proudly. "Remember how you used to hate that?"

"Hate's a strong word, Jerry. Your illiteracy was a mild irritant and nothing more."

"Yeah, guess we had bigger problems than that," Jerry said, staring at a ding in the wall that had been made when Nancy had thrown a frying pan at him. Not that she was violent or temperamental. Far from it. Nancy was probably the most even-tempered person to ever live but even the mildest souls had their breaking point. And being married to Jerry had driven Nancy to hers.

"Jerry, I really don't have any desire to dredge all this old nonsense up. If that's where this is headed, I need to hang up now and…"

"We had a son together," Jerry interrupted. "I can accept that our marriage had failed and we were better off without each other but don't you think we should have at least maintained some positive ties for our kid? Ever think of that?"

Another pause. This time it went on so long that Jerry thought she actually had hung up but she finally responded.

"By the time our marriage had ended, Andy was old enough to make up his own mind about you and what kind of relationship he wanted with you. Blame me all you want but the decision was his."

Jerry wanted to scream at her, tell that was bull shit and it was all her fault. She had turned their son against out of petty spite for their marriage failing but couldn't. Because Nancy was right. About everything.

"How is he?" Jerry managed to say after he fought off the urge to berate the woman who done her best but was ultimately saddled with the Sisyphean task of being married to a mean and impossibly stubborn man.

"He's good," Nancy replied. "Getting married to a lovely woman in three months. And she's expecting."

Jerry's vision became blurred as his eyes filled up with tears. Not tears of joy but tears of anger and humiliation. Not only was he about get a daughter-in-law but also a grandchild. And he would likely never meet either one of them.

"Well, isn't that fucking perfect," he said, his voice hoarse with tears. "Aren't you just the big winner? The doting mom becomes a doting mother-in-law and grandma. And I'm left holding the bag again."

"What bag, Jerry?" Nancy asked, her formerly comforting voice becoming angry and exasperated.

"Like you give a shit now. You certainly didn't when we were married."

"Goodbye, Jerry," she replied, ignoring this statement altogether. "Whatever you're dealing with, I hope you get through it."

"Yeah, I'll bet you do. Lying, two-faced bitch that you are."

"Good night, Jerry. Don't ever call here again."

Now Jerry was mad enough to spit.

"Fuck you!" he bellowed. "Like I'd ever waste my time with this shit again!"

But she had already hung up. And who could blame her? Jerry proceeded to slam the phone down so hard he actually cracked the receiver. Ordinarily a little mindless violence often helped him feel better but tonight all he was left with was a broken phone and the knowledge that it was possible to push your already-estranged family members even further away.

His head began to pound and with no alcohol in the house, Jerry decided to join his farmhands and take another lap around the property. He loaded his old .30-.30 and went outside. He hadn't used the gun in years. During his hunting days, it was his favorite. The site was just a little crooked but Jerry was a crack shot with it. If that thing was stupid enough to come back tonight, Jerry would get it.

"Don't mind me," he called out to his farmhands. "Stay where you are for right now. I'm going to check out the old silo."

His farmhands nodded and maintained their positions. Jerry walked over to the silo and leaned against it, the lights of the house and dairy barn twinkling pleasantly in the distance. The silo had been here when Jerry had purchased the property. He guessed it was around eighty years old or better. Nancy had suggested they tear it down but Jerry opted to keep it up. He liked the sense of history it brought. And if things didn't turn around soon, history would be the only thing Jerry had left.

It was just before midnight when he heard something rustling in tall grass near the silo. Jerry had started to drift off when he had first heard the noise. In his state of half-sleep, his first thought was that Andy was making trouble again. That kid was always goofing off when he should have been doing his chores. It was until Jerry heard the hissing sound that he fully woke up and leapt to his feet.

He pointed the .30-.30 around but didn't see anything. How could he? It was pitch black out. A thick layer of clouds had blanketed the full, stark-white moon. Jerry walked around the silo with the rifle at the ready. He had almost gone completely around when he heard the grass rustling again. He realized it was coming up behind him. He swung the rifle around and pointed it at the grass. Just as he raised the rifle to take aim, something hissed and jumped out at him. Jerry screamed and fell to the ground, the rifle firing wildly into the air. Whatever it was took off running, its breath coming out in strange, panicked chuffs. Jerry readied the rifle again and looked through its crooked scope. At first, he couldn't see anything. Then he could see the round head of the creature bobbing wildly against the lights of the barn. His farmhands were running over and he saw the creature take a hard left. Although his eyesight had gone to hell in the last five years, Jerry followed it with the sight and took aim. It was a moving target but old man or not, Jerry was still a fantastic shot. He squeezed the trigger and the rifle reported loudly in the chilly night. He heard the creature shriek and watched its head disappear from view. He stood up and ran over to it, motioning for his farmhands to come with him.

They arrived at the creature and found it still alive, screeching and desperately trying to drag itself to safety. Bright red blood was pouring from its side and soaking the grass underneath it.

"Jesus, what the hell is that?" one of his farmhands asked, leaning in to get a closer look.

Although Jerry didn't believe it, he knew exactly it was.

A fucking Chupacabra.

Not wanting to dwell on the unreality of the situation any longer, Jerry pointed the .30-.30 at it and pulled the trigger.

After the rifle shot had finished echoing across the open landscape, there was silence. Jerry and his farmhands stared at the mysterious and now dead creature in disbelief.

"Damn, boss," one of them said in awe. "I think this is going to make you rich!"

Jerry smiled, knowing the farmhand was right. He *was* going to be rich.

The three of them were so elated with this knowledge that they didn't hear the low cries of anguish coming from the tall grass directly behind them.

Jerry had never wanted fame but it came regardless after the word about his discovery had spread. While he initially wasn't happy about it, he quickly learned that great reward accompanied his newfound fame. He had been paid a hefty sum for the creature and offers rolled in ranging from book deals to interviews on talk shows. Jerry agreed to most of them (though he turned down interviews with CNN and MSNBC. Liberal hogwash) and while he had to contend with a lot of unwanted visitors coming to his farm, the money he had received allowed him to install high fences and a state-of-the-art security system. After about three months, the excitement died down but Jerry's bank account had grown exponentially and business was better than ever. He had expanded his herd by fifty cows and was able to find reputable help, which meant shit canning the burnouts and ne'er-do-wells he had been stuck with up until that point. He had given them a respectable severance package and although he anticipated some form of petty revenge, nothing had transpired.

Six months after that fateful night, things were still going well for Jerry. Sales of his dairy products were at an all-time high and he was sleeping well. The business he had built from scratch was operating like a Swiss watch and when it had run into trouble, Jerry had saved it.

What else did a man need?

He had a framed a photo of himself holding the creature up by its arm (cropping out the farmhands who done exactly jack shit during that ordeal, of course). It looked feeble and pathetic while Jerry looked like a strong and triumphant warrior. It was hard to believe such a small and inefficient looking thing possessed the preternatural strength to kill an animal three times its size, even if it was something as docile as a cow. Still, the superior species had ultimately triumphed. Jerry would sometimes spend up to twenty minutes marveling at this picture, as well as the slugs they had removed from its body (which Jerry had also framed).

His farmhands were working hard and the trucks were coming and going on an almost daily basis.

Life was good.

Sometime later, Jerry was finishing a perfect dinner of prime rib, grilled asparagus, and garlic mashed potatoes when he heard commotion coming from outside. That gave him pause. He hadn't heard commotion of any kind since installing the fences and the security system. Not only had it deterred intruders, it gave the farm a sense of calm and tranquility that hadn't existed during its most low-key times.

He went into the basement and checked the security monitors but they revealed it was business as usual on his property, at least until he reached the camera that showed the inside of the barn. The animals looked upset.

Something had gotten inside.

Jerry came outside with his rifle to a familiar chorus of agitated mooing. He looked down the driveway at the fence and to his horror; the wires running along the top had been crudely ripped apart. Jerry knew he needed to call the police but he also knew they wouldn't get here in time if something was attacking his cows.

He took a deep breath and headed for the barn. He had killed one of these fuckers before and he could absolutely do it again. He entered the barn to find his cows mooing and crashing against the sides of their stalls. Jerry crept toward the opposite end of the barn and began playing out all the possible scenarios in his head. If it were another Chupacabra, would people give a shit? Would the scrutiny he feared finally happen? Would they shut down his farm so they could test the soil and all the animals and see what it was that drew the strange creatures to it? Jerry had real money now but if he wanted to hold onto it, his business still needed to operate at full capacity.

He walked the entire length of the barn and found nothing out of the ordinary. The cows had actually calmed down by the time he finished checking it. Relieved there was nothing killing his herd, he went back outside. There was still the issue of the fence, though. *Something* had torn it apart. Deciding it was time to call the police, he reached inside his pocket for his phone and that's when heard the hissing sound. Heavy footsteps crunched on the rocky soil behind him and although he tried to ready his rifle, he was too late.

Something with at least six inches on Jerry struck him in the face with roughly the force of a cannon fired at point-blank range. Jerry fell to the ground and felt the rifle fly out his hands. His attacker bent down until it was face to face with Jerry. It was another Chupacabra but this one was at least twice the size of the one Jerry had killed. He had remembered mocking his farmhand for claiming to see a creature this size and he now regretted it. Jerry realized that he was staring into the hissing and foul-smelling face of the smaller creature's parent. It had waited all this time to seek its revenge. And as it gutted Jerry and he felt his insides spill out of him, he briefly mourned the fact that there was nobody who would do the same for him.

The creature stood over Jerry's dead body and let out a triumphant screech before skittering off into the night.

The creature and the rest of its kind were well hidden, but they would need to go elsewhere to find food from now on.

And that was okay.

They had no more business here.

Beware of Dog

"You ready to make some real money?"

The question threw Dustin off at first. Of course he was ready to make some real money. More importantly, he *needed* to make some real money. In addition to his car being repoed, he had also been evicted from his apartment earlier that week. One month of not being able to pay rent quickly became two which inevitably became three. And three strikes meant you were out on your ass. But what the hell was Marco talking about? Another one of his harebrained and misguided get rich quick schemes? Most likely, but fuck it; Dustin could humor his friend for the umpteenth time.

"What kind of real money?" he asked, his eyes already starting to glaze over. Marco talked a good game but did little to follow through on any of it.

"I mean *real* money. It's like you said, the old prick must be sitting on at least a million dollars," Marco answered, causing Dustin to almost choke on his beer. He suddenly understood what Marco was talking about. Old Man Boyle. Marco wanted to rob him. But surely it was just drunk talk.

"Are you serious?" Dustin asked. While it was true he had made the suggestion himself, he had also been severely intoxicated at the time. He didn't think Marco would take it to heart. Plus, it had been over a month ago. If Marco was serious, it would be the longest commitment of his life.

"Why not?" Marco asked as he swallowed the foam that had

collected at the bottom of his Bud Light.

"Because I was drunk when I said that. I didn't mean it."

"Yeah, well, maybe it's time you did because the last time I looked, things weren't going so well for you."

Although Dustin wanted to punch Marco for pointing that out, he was right. Things were bad. And his multiple DUIs pretty much made him unemployable. Well, that and the assault but that was hardly his fault. The kid had come at him with a knife. Or at least that's what it had looked like at the time. The knife in question turned out to be a smartphone but try telling that to a judge when you're on your fourth conviction.

"We've all heard the stories," Marco continued as he motioned for the bartender to bring them another round. "And yet nobody's ever taken the initiative to find out if the stories are true."

Said "stories" were all variations on how Old Man Boyle, the owner of Boyle's Auto Wrecking and Disposal, had supposedly amassed a fortune that placed him somewhere between Mark Zuckerberg and Bill Gates on the rich asshole scale. Some said his father was a famous bootlegger. Others said he ran drugs and guns to and from South America. And some pragmatically suggested it had come from savings and careful investing. A few kooks had even suggested he had a made a deal with the Devil. Dustin didn't know what to believe but there was one thing he did know: Old Man Boyle had money. And a lot of it.

Dustin had been around ten when his father had sold Old Man Boyle the leftover lumber from the deck he had built in their backyard. Dustin had accompanied his father to Boyle's and found the place to be a little scary. Old cars and trucks were piled high around the property like rusting behemoths ready to strike unsuspecting pedestrians (or at least them give them a nasty case of tetanus). Old Man Boyle himself was something to behold. He was a tall man and save for the protruding belly that hung over his grease-stained Dickey's, he was gaunt and had a thick beard that reminded Dustin of ZZ Top. He said almost nothing as he looked over the lumber that Dustin and his father had piled in the back of their old pick-up truck. After staring at it for a solid minute, he finally grunted and pulled out a large wad of cash that made Dustin's jaw drop. He had never seen that much money before and hadn't since. Old Man Boyle counted out a few bills and handed them to Dustin's father.

"Where did he get all that money from, Daddy?" Dustin had asked on their way home.

"Nobody really knows," his father answered cryptically. "But he definitely didn't get it from selling used lumber and old cars."

While not exactly a Rhodes scholar, Dustin's father (dead nine years now from renal failure) was something of autodidact when it came to their town, its history, and its inhabitants. If he thought Old Man Boyle had a fortune stashed away, then it was likely true. But stealing it? That was a horse of a different color. Dustin would need a lot more beer and explaining for that to seem like a good idea

And Marco was more than happy to oblige him.

As it turned out, his plan was pretty simple. Old Man Boyle closed at nine o'clock on the dot. By ten o'clock, he'd be sound asleep with a little help from his friends Jack and Jim. Marco had spent almost the entire month casing the place and although he had been careful not to spend too much time on the actual property, he claimed he could hear Old Man Boyle's buzz saw-like snoring from the street.

"Imagine running a blender at full speed and then turning on a rusty chainsaw. That's what the old prick sounds like," Marco said after their sixth beer. "It's perfect. As long as he's snoring, we'll be able to hear him. So much for him surprising us with a twelve gauge."

"So assuming he has all this money, where does he keep it?" Dustin asked, slowly warming up to the plan.

"I have an idea," Marco said, cracking open a peanut.

"You mean you don't know exactly where it is?" Dustin asked, disappointed.

"Well, the place ain't that big," Marco replied. "I spent some time in the main office about two weeks ago. Told the miserable old shit I was looking for an engine for a '76 Camaro. Ended up buying a set of windshield wipers instead. I paid him and asked to use the bathroom. When I went into the bathroom, he was holding the money. When I came back, he was coming out of the back room and the money was gone."

"Does he have a cash register up front?"

Marco shook his head.

"He's got an old cash box. And do you really think he leaves it full of money when he closes? Of course not. The old prick puts it in a safe, which is obviously out back. Maybe he's got it hidden under the floor or behind a false wall but it won't take us long to find it."

"Security cameras?" Dustin asked, waving the bartender over for a seventh (and likely final) round.

"He's got one at the front gate," Marco answered. "But it's old. It'll take me two seconds to disable it."

He gave Dustin a cocky grin before cracking open another peanut.

"So when does this happen?" Dustin asked, picturing the eviction notice he had found taped to his door the other day.

"Sunday night. We'll watch us some *Rick and Morty* and then we'll get fucking paid. How's that sound?

Dustin took a big gulp of his beer. He thought it sounded wonderful.

It was after one when he got back to his uncle's house. Dustin didn't have much contact with his family these days but his uncle was all right. While he stressed to Dustin this wasn't going to be a permanent arrangement, he could at least stay there until he got on his feet again. Dustin wondered how much it would please his uncle to know said day was coming much faster than either of them expected. Dustin knew he'd have to disappear after he got the money, which would prevent a proper goodbye. He decided he'd leave his uncle ten grand as a thank you.

It was the least he could do.

Sunday night arrived and Dustin, as per Marco's instructions, was dressed in all black. When he arrived at Marco's house, he was disturbed by a couple of things. One was the shiny pistol resting on the scuffed coffee table and the other was Marco. He was high.

"You ready to make some money, man?" he slurred at Dustin in a voice that sounded thick and sleepy.

Dustin couldn't believe it. They hadn't even left the house yet and the whole thing was in danger of falling apart. He stared into Marco's watery and sanguine eyes and wondered if it was too late to back out. He certainly wasn't on the line for anything illegal yet but how would Marco react? Would he get violent? It was hard to say. Marco could be pretty nasty when he was intoxicated but so could Dustin. It's partly what made them such a delightful pair. Dustin watched as Marco carefully placed a crow bar, a small drill, bolt cutters, a chisel, and a variety of other small tools into a black canvas duffel bag. When he finished, he zipped it up and tossed Dustin a ski mask.

"Let's go," he said, tucking the pistol into his waistband.

Dustin weighed his options. Walk away now and spend the rest of his life in poverty or roll the dice and retire early?

He opted for the latter.

They parked Marco's old Ford three blocks away from Boyle's. They were in a part of town where all the other businesses had dried up and died years ago. Boyle's was the only thing still standing. It was a relief not to have worry about any witnesses but there was still something unsettling about the area. If Boyle really had money, why hadn't he relocated to a better part of town? Why keep your business in the middle of a decaying industrial graveyard?

As they walked up the long driveway to Boyle's, Dustin could hear the unmistakable sound of loud snoring. Marco wasn't kidding. The guy sounded like a jackhammer. Marco turned to Dustin with a lopsided smile on his face.

"I hope he's having sweet dreams. Cause he ain't going to be feeling too good when he wakes up in the morning."

Dustin felt a stab of nervousness in his gut.

"What do you mean?" he asked.

"I mean he's going to pretty upset when he finds out we robbed him blind," Marco replied. "What else would I be talking about?"

Dustin relaxed a little but also imagined a stoned and keyed-up Marco using his crowbar on Old Man Boyle's skull once they had finished the job. And there was no amount of money that was worth a murder one rap.

Dustin's trepidation grew even bigger when they reached the front gate. There was a rusted sign hanging up that had probably been there since the Nixon administration. It was a sign Dustin had seen a hundred times in front of a hundred different properties but he had never paid it much mind. It consisted of three simple words that seemed especially foreboding in their current situation:

"Beware of Dog"

Dustin kept his eyes on the rusting sign as Marco went to work on the camera that was perched above the gate. He took out his wire cutters and made a couple of quick snips, prompting the red light on top of the camera to turn off. They were all set.

"What are you gawking at?" he whispered at Dustin, who pointed at the sign.

"You didn't say anything about a dog!" he exclaimed.

"That's because there isn't one," Marco replied as he began to lower himself inside the main grounds.

"Are you sure?" Dustin asked. He knew that an aggressive

Doberman or German Shepherd could make short work of a person, even a big one. And he and Marco weren't exactly Dwayne Johnson when it came to strength and physical stature.

"Positive," Marco said as he jumped down. "Now get the fuck over here."

Although the sign had made him a little uneasy, Dustin knew there was no turning back. He was already an accessory to breaking and entering and knew damn well that if Marco was caught, he'd drop the dime on him without hesitation. So sign be damned, Dustin scaled the gate and landed on the ground next to Marco.

"Where to?"

Marco pointed at the small, ramshackle building in the middle of the yard and they began to walk, their feet crunching on gravel and bits of broken glass. They were almost to the front door when Dustin heard something in the distance. Although Old Man Boyle's snoring was still operating at roughly the same volume as an AC/DC concert, Dustin could swear it was a footstep. And a big one at that.

"Did you hear something?" he whispered as he grabbed Marco's arm.

"All I can hear is that fucking old man doing his best impression of a busted lawn mower."

"Something's out there!" Dustin insisted.

"Bull shit! Now stand guard, I'm going inside."

Dustin's heart began to pound. He watched as Marco used his crow bar to pop open the front door. He disappeared inside and Dustin scanned the yard but everything was still. No signs of life, animal or human. The song of Old Man Boyle's snoring continued, its rhythm jagged and abrasive.

Five minutes went by with no sign of Marco. If the safe was anything like the rest of the junkyard, it probably wouldn't take very long to crack but Dustin also realized he had no concept of how long it took to crack a safe, easy or hard. Either way, he decided it was time to check on Marco. He went inside the main office, which smelled like stale farts and motor oil. He crept into the back room and saw a wide-open safe that was surrounded by Marco's tools. Dustin peeked inside and saw it was empty. Had the miserable son of a bitch bailed on him and left him hanging? Just as he began to seethe with anger, he felt a hand on his shoulder. He jumped and turned to see Marco standing behind him.

"What the fuck? I told you to stand guard!" he hissed at Dustin.

"You were gone a long time," Dustin replied shakily. "I thought maybe something had happened."

"Like what? That old bastard sucking me up through his nose? Get real."

"Whatever," Dustin said, eager for the whole fucking thing to be over. "Did you get the money?"

Marco smiled and held up the duffel bag. Dustin looked inside and saw stacks of bills, most of them large denominations. He hadn't seen that much money since the last time he had visited Boyle's.

"And that's not all. Check this out."

He walked Dustin over to a cabinet that contained numerous bottles of booze, most of them completely full.

"Old Grand Dad whiskey!" Marco whispered excitedly. "My grandfather used to drink that shit. It's classic!"

"Don't we have enough money to buy our own booze now?" Dustin asked.

Marco scoffed.

"Fuck that, man, why pay for it when we can get it for free? Go back outside. I'm going to bag this shit up."

Dustin didn't see the point of stealing thirty-year-old whiskey but he also knew they were on the home stretch. Just a few more minutes and his problems would be over. He started outside but stopped when something else caught his eye. It was a serious of bizarre and ominous-looking symbols that had been painted on the far wall. He looked closer and saw the symbols were painted using a dark brown color. He felt a chill when he remembered that blood dried brown. And didn't one of the rumors about Old Man Boyle suggest he had made a deal with the Devil? Dustin continued to study the symbols and found them as hypnotic as he did repulsive.

"What are you doing?" Marco asked, snapping Dustin out of the mild trance he had fallen into.

"Look at these!" Dustin said, motioning toward the symbols. "What do you think they are?"

"Who gives a shit? We've got the money. Now go outside and keep watch. Unless you want to ask the cops what they think."

Although Dustin badly wanted to know what the symbols were, Marco was right. He walked outside and listened to Old Man Boyle's snoring, which suddenly didn't sound so abrasive.

The minutes ticked by and Marco didn't come out. Dustin didn't like that at all. How long did it take to bag up a few bottles of booze? Just as Dustin was about to check on him, he heard something. What sounded like a footstep before was now a muffled thud. And that muffled thud became a sickening wet ripping sound. Dustin was so distracted by the awful sounds coming out of the office that he didn't even notice that Old Man Boyle had stopped snoring.

"Marco?" he called out, his heart ready to leap out of his chest. Silence again. Just as Dustin was about to run, he felt something heavy bounce off his chest. He looked down and saw it was Marco's severed head, its face locked in a permanent state of abject terror. Dustin screamed and began to run for the front gate. He had made it barely ten feet when a gunshot rang out and struck him in the small of the back, instantly obliterating his spine. He fell to the ground with no sensation below his waist. The only thing he could feel was the hot blood escaping from his body. Bright spots danced in front of his eyes as he slowly began to lose consciousness. Footsteps approached and Dustin saw Old Man Boyle standing over him with a nasty smile on his face.

"Should have obeyed the sign, boy."

"Dog!" Dustin gasped. It was the only word he could manage to say at that moment.

Old Man Boyle threw back his head and laughed.

"Well, it ain't quite a dog," he replied. "Ain't exactly sure what it is but it does the job. Did you really think you two assholes were the first ones to try and rob me? Far from it. But don't worry. My pet is very thorough. Ain't gonna be nothin' left of you when he's finished."

Old Man Boyle then proceeded to say something in a language that Dustin didn't recognize. Almost immediately, he heard a vicious growl and felt hot breath against the side of his face as acidic saliva began to corrode his skin. He was fading fast and before everything went black, he saw only teeth.

And they were big.

The next day arrived and Old Man Boyle opened for business at eight o'clock sharp, like he had done every day without fail for almost forty years. Even if he had earned his fortune through non-traditional (and somewhat unearthly) means, he had still earned it. And nobody was going to take that away from him. He cleared his throat and expectorated a wad of thick black mucus that sizzled when it hit the ground. As he opened up the front gate to prepare for the morning deliveries, he could hear his pet snoring softly nearby. It was satisfied.

And as Old Man Boyle watched the morning sun blanket his little kingdom, he decided he was, too.

Lee Marvin Settles a Score

"You're boring."

Those were her exact words. Ten years of marriage, numerous trips around the world, and every possible material possession she could want and that's how it ended. The words were bad enough but the delivery was what really drove the stake into Alan's heart. She said it off-handedly as if commenting on the weather. She didn't care about him in the least and only gave him an explanation because he had begged her to. And even then it was just a way for her to get out the door and run off with her new boyfriend. Alan wanted to hate both of them but couldn't quite bring himself to do it. The fact was Alan really *was* boring. And that hurt worst of all.

"Bull shit!"

He was at Applebee's with his friend Tom and they were halfway through their meal when Alan realized even his favorite restaurants were boring. It was amazing his marriage had lasted ten years and not ten weeks. Alan stared at his half-eaten steak salad and wondered how he made it to forty-two and not realized he was roughly as exciting as a trip to Home Depot.

"Did you hear me?" Tom asked with his piercing blue eyes trained on Alan. "That's bull shit. You're boring? Her favorite movie is *Dirty Dancing*! How can you get more boring than that?"

Alan didn't really have an answer. His favorite movie was *The Godfather*, which was about as cliché as you could get.

"Here's what you need to do," Tom said taking a sip of his impossibly tall glass of Blue Moon. "Take a trip to Miami or Cabo, get piss drunk every night, and fuck anything that'll have you. Then when you come back, I'll have Maggie introduce you to some of her friends. She knows a few divorcees and let me tell you, those chicks are wild. If I weren't married…"

Tom chuckled before eating another bite of his rib eye.

Alan continued to stare down at his steak salad. He knew Tom meant well and while his suggestions weren't bad, the only thing Alan wanted to do was curl up like a pill bug and never face daylight or people again. They'd only serve to disappoint him.

And given how boring he was, he didn't have anything to offer anybody anyway.

When he got home from dinner, he flipped on the television and saw *Point Blank* was on Turner Classic Movies. Alan had seen the film years back and enjoyed it but hadn't thought much about it since. As he watched Lee Marvin kick the shit out of anybody who crossed his path and pissed him off, Alan bemoaned his own beta male status. He understood they were only movies and nobody actually lived like that but he still wanted one bad ass Lee Marvin moment. Just one. It wouldn't be to win his wife back or impress anybody; it would just be for his own satisfaction. It had been a long time since Alan had really done anything for himself.

He made a point to watch a different Lee Marvin film every night over the next week. He couldn't remember the last time he had total control over the television. He started his marathon with *Hell in the*

Pacific. The night after that he watched *Emperor of the North.* He decided to go with something lighter on Thursday and watched *Cat Ballou,* which had Marvin playing two different roles. Alan learned he had won an Academy Award for that and it was well deserved (at least in his humble opinion). Friday night brought *The Dirty Dozen* (as well as a six-pack of Budweiser) and Alan ended the marathon on Saturday with *Shout at the Devil.* The films were entertaining and provided a nice distraction from everything else that was going on. That made it a win for Alan but the best was yet to come.

He was at the grocery store the next day trying to decide which Hungry Man TV dinner to buy. They weren't his favorite, but they happened to be on sale for a dollar ninety-eight each. He could cover his whole week for less than ten bucks and given how his ex-wife was likely going to clean him out once the divorce was official, he needed to be mindful of such things.

He finally decided on the meatloaf and as he pulled it out of the freezer, he felt somebody crash into him, sending not only the TV dinner flying but his entire basket of groceries as well. He winced as he heard the sound of his strawberry preserves hitting the ground and shattering.

Wonderful, he thought. *Anything else, universe? Can my car break down, too?*

"Oh my God, I'm so sorry," said the panicked female voice behind him. She sounded young. It was probably some brat teenager too busy texting to notice the world around her.

"It's fine," Alan sighed, finally turning to face her. And when he saw her, all the bull shit from the last couple of months instantly disappeared.

She was perfect.

Her name was Claudia and after she finished apologizing profusely, Alan managed to stumble into an actual conversation with her. He had never been good at talking to women. The only reason he had successfully courted his wife was because they had worked together, which allowed their relationship to develop naturally. Still, Claudia seemed genuinely interested in what he had to say and was even impressed when he told her he was a bank manager.

"Manager?" she said, raising her immaculately groomed eyebrows. "So you're the boss?"

The board of directors might disagree with that slightly but he told her yes, for all intents and purposes, he was the boss.

"Wow, so what's a handsome, successful man like you doing eating this crap?" she asked, motioning toward the TV dinner section.

He could tell her the truth but then it would be all over before it even started. He didn't know much about women but he knew revealing the bleak aspects of your life early on spelled death if you wanted things to progress.

"Well, it's a nice change of pace from eating filet mignon and caviar every night," he replied.

It wasn't much of a response but Claudia threw back her head and laughed like it was the funniest thing she had ever heard.

"You're cute," she said, gently brushing his arm.

Alan practically jumped when she did that. Was this woman really interested? It didn't make sense but then he heard Tom's voice in his head, clear as a bell:

"Fucking go for it, you idiot! Do you think women like her normally hook up with guys they meet in the grocery store? This is some once-in-a-lifetime shit you've got going on! If I weren't married, I'd be all over that!"

Alan was so caught up in his imaginary admonishing from Tom that he missed the next thing Claudia said.

"What?" he asked, allowing himself to snap back to reality.

"I asked if you wanted to go have a drink with me," she said, looking at him intently with her creamy jade eyes.

"Tonight?"

"No time like the present," she said, her pouty lips curling into a mischievous smile.

Alan returned the smile and told her that would be great.

No time like the present, indeed.

The next week was the wildest one of Alan's life. Claudia wasn't big on conversation but that hardly mattered when the sex was so constant and exhausting it didn't leave them the time or energy for anything else. They spent most of their time in various motels around town. He had taken two weeks off from work (which were long overdue) and while his rendezvous with Claudia were mainly relegated to the day, his evenings also had a newfound energy. He repainted the entire house in an effort to remove any final traces of his soon-to-be ex. She had decided to paint the living room a garish teal and Alan had always hated it but never had the gumption to speak up. It was nice to finally get it back to normal, especially considering he had bought the house before they had even met. He punctuated these painting sessions with his old vinyl collection and some marijuana he had gotten from one of the security guards at work. And it was quality stuff. Frank Zappa's *Sheik Yerbouti* had never sounded so good. As he painted away the last of his ex-wife's terrible taste, he realized things were finally looking up.

There was one catch, though.

"She's married?" Tom asked.

They were having dinner at a sushi place that had recently opened up. If it was good, Alan planned on asking Claudia if she wanted to go for a little post-coital sashimi. Applebee's no longer cut it.

"Yeah," Alan said. "But I don't know the guy."

"So what? You're cheating with somebody else's wife. Have you forgotten what just happened to you?"

"She wasn't cheating on me," Alan said.

Tom's look became one of weary disgust.

"Do you really believe that?"

"I mean, I don't think they did anything before she left," Alan insisted and Tom rolled his eyes.

"Either way, think about how that made you feel. Are you really okay with doing that to someone else?"

Alan pictured a feeble-looking schlub, not unlike himself weeping uncontrollably behind the steering wheel of an Acura or Camry (or something equally lame). Then he pictured Claudia. Limber, luscious Claudia.

"Yes," he said before shoving a few chunks of sushi into his mouth. It was good but not Claudia good. He'd have to figure out somewhere else to take her.

Tom shook his head.

"You're playing with fire, buddy."

And Alan knew Tom was right. But he didn't care.

Two days later he was headed to Claudia's house for the first time. It was located outside of town and was a little more modest than Alan had anticipated. He didn't think beautiful women like her ever lived in houses like this. It was two stories, white, and while it wasn't in bad shape (the porch steps they had walked up were new), it struck Alan as a starter home, something a young couple would live in until they could afford somewhere better. It looked like Claudia and her husband had never reached that point.

"It belonged to his parents," she explained as she turned the key in the lock. "My husband lived here his whole life and I moved in right after we got married. After his parents died two years ago, it officially became ours."

Alan wondered how someone as gorgeous as Claudia would ever agree to such an arrangement. Was there an unplanned pregnancy? That seemed reasonable but in one of the rare moments where she opened up, Claudia said she didn't have any kids. Alan hoped she hadn't lied to him. And if so, what else had she held back?

The inside of the house was also well kept but the furniture was too old and tasteless to be anything but a remnant of the 70s. The only modern thing in the living room was a high-definition television. To Alan, that screamed she had married somebody in a perpetual state of arrested development. A grown man who couldn't be bothered to update his living space save for a television to watch sports and action movies on was clearly still a boy. The whole thing didn't make any sense and for the first time since his whirlwind romance with Claudia began, Alan was uneasy.

"Are you sure he's not coming back until tomorrow?"

"Positive," Claudia said, flipping through the mail that was on the coffee table. As far as Alan could tell, it was mostly junk, save for issues of *Maxim* and *High Times*. Alan wanted to laugh but kept quiet. Nothing good would come from him openly mocking Claudia's husband.

"Where did he go?" Alan asked, envisioning a mulleted man in a sleeveless Iron Maiden t-shirt roaring down the highway in an old Camaro with his buddies while they sucked down Coors Lights by the case. A hunting trip perhaps? Alan shuddered at thought of that. If the guy was a gun nut, that could mean serious trouble for everyone involved.

"His boss sent him to Pittsburg to pick up some auto parts," Claudia explained, tossing the useless mail into a Buffalo Bills garbage can that was parked next to the television.

"So he works?" Alan blurted out before he could stop himself.

"Yeah, he had to get a job to keep up with the taxes and utilities after he inherited the house," Claudia said in a casual tone, either unaware of the implication of Alan's question or just indifferent to it.

"Oh, yeah, most people don't realize how expensive it is to own a house, even if it's handed down to you," Alan babbled. "We had a guy a few years ago who inherited this beautiful mansion from his uncle. And when he found out what the property tax was, he went nuclear and came in to talk to me about it. I explained to him that I'm not a lawyer…"

He stopped when he saw how completely disinterested Claudia was with his story. He was becoming boring again. The only thing this woman wanted to do was fuck and forget about the loser she was married to for a few hours each day.

And Alan was more than happy to accommodate her.

The bedroom Claudia selected looked like a guest bedroom to Alan. There was a lumpy queen bed in the middle of the room and a picture of the Virgin Mary hanging on the wall. It was clearly the decorating scheme of an old lady. Alan was surprised again at how little Claudia and her husband had done to make the house their own.

"So," Claudia said. "Here we are."

Alan pointed at the picture of Mary.

"Don't you think we should turn that away?"

Claudia laughed but Alan saw something flash in her eyes that he didn't like at all. It looked like fear.

"No way," she said. "We have to leave everything as is. Hubby's orders."

"Oh," Alan said lamely. He didn't know what else to say.

"So are you going to stand there worrying about a stupid painting or are you going to fuck me?"

It was a fair question. Alan decided to go with the latter.

After the third round had ended, Alan needed to use the bathroom.

"Right there," Claudia said sleepily, pointing to a door across the room. When they first entered, Alan had assumed it was a closet.

He stood up and opened the door to reveal a cramped bathroom that was about six feet wide and eight feet long. If you were sitting on the toilet (which Alan had no interest in doing), your feet would be resting in the tiny shower directly across from it.

Alan removed his throbbing genitals from his underwear and voided into the toilet bowl, which despite being old was spotlessly clean. He also noticed a lavender Yankee candle and a Bic lighter on top of the tank. Alan guessed that aside from the television, the candle was the newest thing in the house.

He supposed that keeping everything clean and fresh smelling was Claudia's way of having some form of control in her life. That and fucking boring guys in the throes of a midlife crisis. Either way, things were working out well for Alan.

At least until he heard the front door open.

"Claude!" Alan heard a voice bellow from downstairs. He froze. He had been in the middle of washing his hands with the tiny sliver of white soap that sat next to the faucet and laughing to himself about what a rube Claudia's husband was. Now he felt guilty and even a little scared. There was no possible way this could end well.

"Claude!" came the voice again. He didn't sound especially intimidating but if he had a gun, it didn't matter if he sounded like Mickey Mouse. The trajectory of the bullet would still be the same.

"Be right down!" he heard Claudia answer as she jumped out of bed. Alan listened as she threw on her clothes and in another few seconds, she was at the door to the bathroom.

"Just stay in here and be quiet," she whispered to him. "I'll take care of it."

Alan didn't respond and Claudia hovered outside the door, which was mildly annoying. Did she expect a response? After a few more brutal seconds, he finally saw the shadows of her feet disappear from the under the doorway. He heard her footsteps padding down the stairs to greet her cuckolded and potentially homicidal husband.

The two of them began speaking but Alan couldn't make out what they were saying. If Claudia could get the guy to go out for pizza or some kind of take-out, Alan could escape with no problem. There was the issue of not having his car there. Claudia had driven them there in her aging Mazda hatchback. Alan would have to walk for a while before calling for a Lyft car to give him a ride back to town. He just hoped the driver wouldn't mind picking up him next to a cornfield or whatever random landmark he'd be stuck in front of. But that was the least of his problems at the moment. He still needed to get out of the house with his balls intact.

Another agonizing couple of minutes passed before he heard footsteps coming up the stairs. To his horror, the footsteps didn't belong to Claudia, but her husband.

"You can't tell me where to go in own damn house, you numb cunt!"

And it was at that point Alan knew he was going to die.

"Are you hiding something from me, girl?" Claudia's husband asked.

"Of course not!" she replied. "I just didn't have a chance to clean this room. I know how neat you like everything."

"Damn straight I do. And what's that smell? It almost smells like…"

He stopped talking and Alan listened as he shuffled through the sheets on the bed before letting out a triumphant cry.

"Ah ha! Whose fucking pants are these then?"

"They're mine!" Claudia said. "I like to wear them around the house!"

"Since when do you wear men's khakis around the house? Are really pulling this shit on me again, girl?"

Again? Alan thought, wanting to scream. Everything in his life prior to this point had been a vacation. Being a boring unpopular kid who grew up to be a boring unpopular adult, the divorce, the self-loathing, all of that was incidental compared to what was unfolding a mere five feet away from him. And the only thing protecting him from an irate husband was a paper-thin door that wouldn't stop a strong rainfall let alone a bullet. Alan's thoughts went back to Lee Marvin, who would have already exited the bathroom and kicked this asshole's teeth in. He wanted his Lee Marvin moment more than ever but it was looking less and less likely.

"So where's he hiding?" the husband asked.

"He went out the back door when you came in. He's in the woods somewhere."

The husband laughed.

"So I'm looking for a guy with no pants running around in my daddy's woods like a dumb ass?"

"Yes," Claudia replied. "So go find him and do what you have to do."

"What have I told you about telling me my business, bitch?"

The statement was immediately followed by a slap so hard Alan could feel the reverberations inside the bathroom. He heard Claudia cry out in pain and start to sob. The fear and despair Alan was experiencing became clouded with self-hatred for his cowardice. He badly wanted to take action but instead stayed quiet and shook like a frightened rabbit.

A very boring frightened rabbit.

Claudia's sobbing continued as her husband went into the hallway to make a phone call. Alan couldn't hear what he was saying but he assumed the bastard was calling for backup, which could be good news. If they were off looking in the woods for him, Alan could take Claudia and leave. Maybe take her to the police and have the son of a bitch thrown in jail for assault.

Claudia's sobbing became louder and Alan looked down to see the shadow of her feet at the door.

"I hate him so much," she said, her voice a husky whisper.

Alan didn't reply but she continued talking.

"I just wish we were back in one of those motels. We could make love and then you could hold me and tell me how everything's going to be okay. Doesn't that sound nice, Josh?"

"Josh?" Alan asked. "Do you seriously not know my name?"

"I meant Alan!" she exclaimed. "I said Josh because you kind of look like Josh Groban and…"

"Oh, Jesus Christ," Alan interrupted, feeling very foolish. She was never seriously interested in him. It was all just a game to her. And Alan wasn't going to be the winner.

He heard the husband's footsteps enter the room but Claudia still didn't move.

"I've got Kurt and Phil on their way. If your little friend is out there, we'll find him," the asshole said.

There was a lengthy pause and Alan could practically hear the gears turning in the husband's head as he pieced everything together.

"You gotta take a shit?" he asked before letting out a surprisingly high-pitched laugh.

Claudia shifted her feet slightly but stayed by the door.

"Don't tell me he's in there," the husband said, the good humor in his voice dissolving into something decidedly more menacing. "Don't even tell me he's hiding in my daddy's bathroom."

Boots clomped across the room and the doorknob turned several times but Alan had locked it. He always locked the door when he was in the bathroom. It was something his ex-wife used to get on his case about.

"What if you slip and fall or have a heart attack?" she'd ask him. "I don't have the strength to break it down and by the time the ambulance arrived, you might already be dead!"

No, I'm not dead yet, sweetie, Alan thought. *But I will be soon.*

"Hey buddy," the husband called out, knocking softly on the door. "Open the door and come out. You want to desecrate the house my mommy and daddy built from scratch, you should at least have the courage to come out and face me. What kind of a chicken shit are you?"

Likely the biggest one you'll ever meet, Alan mourned to himself.

The husband knocked again and Claudia said something that was too quiet for Alan to hear.

"Shut up, twat," the husband said, putting a particularly strong emphasis on the last word.

He knocked again.

"So are you coming out so we can settle this like a couple of men?"

Alan remained silent and turned his attention to the window. They were on the second floor but it wasn't that high up. Maybe there was a way he could jump down without breaking any bones. He started to open the window when he saw headlights appear on the gravel driveway. The husband's backup had arrived. If they saw him hanging from the window, he'd be the easiest target ever. And after they finished him off, they'd split a case of Keystone and spend the rest of the evening laughing about how weak and pathetic he was. It would be a fitting end to an otherwise unremarkable life. And Tom had warned him, so it wasn't like he didn't deserve it.

Alan sighed and sat down on the toilet.

He wasn't going anywhere.

Alan looked out the window a few minutes later to see Kurt and Phil stationed outside the window smoking cigarettes and splitting a bottle of Jim Beam. Alan wondered if he could make a break for it if they got drunk enough but then he realized guys like them would have to drink a tanker truck worth of booze before they suffered any ill effects. They were the size of linebackers and dressed head to toe in grease-stained denim. They didn't say anything, which was a minor miracle. Their presence was intimidating enough without adding taunts and threats into the mix. Claudia's husband was a different story.

"I just want you to know that when you come out, I'm going to cut your balls off and then your dick. After that, I'll probably move on to your ears and then maybe your nose. Stuff that'll hurt like hell but not kill you right away. What do you say to that, partner?"

Alan didn't answer him. What could he say to that?

"So what are you waiting for?" the husband continued. "I'm running out of patience and you've got no right being in my daddy's bathroom!"

There he is going on about his parents again, Alan thought. *It's like he's already forgotten I fucked his wife. Or he just doesn't care.*

That realization gave Alan an idea. He reached for the toilet paper and began to unspool it from the roll. He was halfway through when he heard a light tapping on the bathroom door.

"Warriors, come out and play-ay-ya!" Claudia's husband taunted as he continued to tap his fingers against the wood.

As unnerving as that was, Alan finished unspooling the toilet paper and placed it in the sink before setting fire to it with the lighter. He took a hand towel from the rack and wrapped it around his face as the room slowly filled with smoke. It didn't take long before the tiny space with thick with it, causing Alan to cough uncontrollably as tears squirted out of his burning eyes. The towel had done jack shit to protect him. If the husband didn't make a move soon, Alan would pass out and probably die. The toilet paper was mostly burnt up but the dense cloud of smoke refused to dissipate. Just as Alan began to feel lightheaded, he heard the miserable bastard's panicked voice call out from the other side of the door.

"Is that fucking smoke? What are you doing to my daddy's bathroom?"

"Why don't you come in and find out, you fucking dick head?" Alan managed to croak out in between coughs.

"You son of a bitch!"

A series of heavy thuds followed before the door gave way and opened, revealing the silhouette of Claudia's husband, barely visible through the smoke. Alan thought back to a scene in *Point Blank* where Lee Marvin smashed a thug in the face with a bottle before the guy could even finish lighting his cigarette. Knowing he'd need to make a similar split-second decision to survive, Alan removed the heavy ceramic lid from the toilet tank and brought it down as hard as he could on the man's head. There was a wet crack and Claudia's husband let out an agonized scream as he collapsed to the ground. The door being open allowed most of the smoke to waft out, giving Alan his first clear look at the man. He didn't look scary at all. He was paunchy with an almost boyish face that reminded Alan of Philip Seymour Hoffman. He didn't know if the man was dead or not and he likely would have continued to gawk at him if it hadn't been for Claudia.

"Larry! Oh my God!" she screamed rushing to his side. She knelt down next to him and began stroking his head, which had a fair amount of blood flowing from it.

"What did you do?" she shrieked at Alan.

Alan didn't respond and only stared at the woman he no longer recognized. There was no sign of joy or affection anywhere on her face. There was only rage from Alan hurting or possibly even killing the man she truly loved. The good news was that it made saying goodbye much easier. Alan noticed a pistol tucked in Larry's waistband and decided to take it for protection. As he bent down to pick it up, something hard smacked him in the side of the head. He dropped back and after he regained his bearings, he saw Claudia standing over him holding the lavender Yankee candle that had sat on the top of the toilet. Alan knew the romance was over but he couldn't believe she had hit him. She raised the candle up again and Alan realized she planned on finishing him off. He grabbed Larry's pistol and pointed it at her. She bared her teeth in response.

"You don't have the balls," she hissed.

Under normal circumstances, she'd have been right. But her husband was just a few inches away from her, dead or at least badly wounded. And Alan never would have guessed he had that in him.

"You sure about that?" he asked her.

"Positive," she replied. "And when Kurt and Phil come in here and see what you did, they're going to kill you. Because you're nothing! That's why your wife left you. You're no man, you're just..."

And that was when Alan squeezed the trigger.

The gunshot was still echoing in Alan's ears as Claudia fell to the ground. Once the ringing had subsided, Alan stood up with the gun still pointed at her. She was facedown and quivering, surrounded by chunks of plaster from the wall behind her. The bullet had landed about three inches to her right. He had never meant to shoot her. Or so he told himself.

He sat for a minute and listened as she quietly snuffed and sobbed.

He tried to think of one final thing to say to her but nothing came to mind.

It was over.

Alan went downstairs and entered the living room just as the front door burst open. It was Kurt and Phil, unarmed save for the almost empty bottle of Jim Beam one of them was clutching.

"Larry! What's going on? Are you okay?"

It took them a second to see Alan standing across the room with Larry's pistol pointed at them. They narrowed their eyes at him.

"Where's Larry?"

"Taking a nap," came Alan's curt reply. He saw a small hook next to the door with a set of keys hanging from it. He walked over with the gun still trained on Kurt and Phil and removed the keys from the hook with a crisp jingle

"You ain't takin' our friend's truck," Kurt or Phil said, in a weak attempt to sound tough.

"What's going to happen if I do?" Alan asked, pointing the gun at the man's head.

"We're gonna fuck you up real bad," the man replied. "What do you think about that?"

Alan raised the gun and smacked him in the face, causing the man to scream and collapse to the ground with blood squirting out of his nose. Alan turned the gun toward the man whose face was still in one piece.

"How about you? Got anything you'd like to say?"

The man kept his mouth shut. He knew who was in charge.

Kurt or Phil led Alan into the garage, where an aging pickup truck waited. It was hard to tell what the color had been, as it was mostly all primer now. He had his doubts it was even going to start but it fired up as soon as he turned the key. He rolled down the window to address Kurt or Phil.

"When Larry wakes up, let him know his truck is going to be in the parking lot of the Home Depot next to the mall. The keys will be under the seat but I'm keeping the gun. I'm sure you can understand why."

Kurt or Phil shot him a look so sour Alan could practically taste it. He threw the truck into gear and peeled down the driveway in a triumphant blaze of glory.

As Alan drove back to town, he reflected on everything that had happened since his wife left him. He would have never guessed he'd end up in a situation like this, but he was profoundly grateful he had. His brush with death meant he finally got to have his Lee Marvin moment.

How many boring people could claim that?

Glad Tidings

It was a week before Christmas and Helen Kennedy's life was on the line. While this wasn't exactly something she relished, it wasn't for naught, either. It was for the kid and Helen would do just about anything for her. That included braving one of the worst blizzards in years in hopes of finding Baby Gumdrop. There was a hot ticket item every year and Baby Gumdrop was the designated one for this season. Helen didn't entirely get it; as far as she could tell Baby Gumdrop was like every other doll on the market save for the packaging and her outfit. The doll was sheathed in what was conceivably supposed to be a gumdrop but to Helen, the bright red vinyl dome on top of Baby Gumdrop's head made her look like the world's smallest member of Devo. Still, it's what the kid wanted and after what had been a particularly difficult year, Helen felt she owed it to her. The kid was a trooper and despite the various emotional and financial hardships they faced on the regular, the kid never had a negative word to say about any of it. If that didn't warrant an ugly doll that ran fifty bucks, Helen didn't know what did. The problem was that every little girl in America wanted Baby Gumdrop and despite spending three weeks checking every online retailer and brick and mortar store in the tri-county area, the fucking thing was nowhere to be found. Sure, there were heartless and opportunistic pricks selling it on Amazon and eBay for upwards of seven hundred dollars but Helen didn't have that kind of money to spend. The retail price itself was something of a strain considering Helen had spent a good portion of the year unemployed and living with her mother. It was only within the last two months she had gotten a job as a proofreader at a law firm and been able to get her and the kid their own place. Her salary was decent enough for the area they were living in but Helen was still wading through student loans and several credit cards she had fallen horribly behind on. When you factored in all that and the never-ending cost of having a five-year-old child as a single parent, twenty-one dollars an hour suddenly seemed downright paltry. But none of that mattered. It was Christmas and the kid was going to get her present.

Helen guaranteed it.

By the time Helen arrived at the mall, the blizzard had reached out whiteout conditions. She struggled to find a parking spot and at one point ran over a huge bump that she couldn't be sure wasn't a body. Despite the cataclysmic weather, the lot was almost full. Helen wondered how many of the cars belong to desperate parents like herself, clinging to the fool's hope that they might find the remaining Baby Gumdrop in one of the mall's two stores that still had a toy section. Undeterred by these terrible odds, Helen stepped out of the warmth of her twelve-year-old Honda and into the harsh and unforgiving night.

Helen's first stop was Target. She had been to roughly a dozen over the last three weeks and all of them had turned up bupkis. And true to form, this Target was no exception. The shelf that once held Baby Gumdrop had been picked clean hours ago, probably by parents who weren't saddled with a job that kept you late and required you to wear pantyhose. Although she knew it was a futile gesture, Helen approached a portly girl dressed in the red t-shirt and khakis that identified her as an employee.

"Baby Gumdrop?" she asked the girl, feebly pointing at the shelf.

"We're out," the employee answered with an indifferent shrug. "They'll send us more but I have no idea when."

Helen forced a smile and thanked the girl. Toys R Us was her next stop. She envisioned herself entering the store and finding one lone Baby Gumdrop waiting for her. She'd pluck it from the shelf and bring it to the register, where a smiling employee would congratulate Helen on her good fortune. It would be perfect. Too perfect to actually occur in reality but Helen hiked across the mall in heels that made her feet swell and throb with each step. The kid was getting that fucking doll. Helen didn't know how or when but it was going to fucking happen.

Just try and stop her.

"We got a big shipment in at nine this morning and it was gone in ten minutes," said the pimple-faced Toys R Us employee. He was at least apologetic but that did little to soothe the anger and desperation Helen was feeling. It was a fucking doll. Why was the universe being so cruel about it?

"And I'm guessing you have no clue when the next shipment is coming in?" she asked the employee.

"They don't tell me anything," he said with a sheepish smile. "That sort of thing is above my pay grade."

Although Helen could relate, now was not the time for solidarity. She left the store, racking her exhausted brain for ideas. Could she borrow money from her mother and pay the exorbitant online fee for the doll? Burn through the one credit card she had left that wasn't maxed out? None of those seemed especially desirable but her options were becoming fewer by the day. And Helen had promised the kid. What choice did she have?

"Baby Gumdrop?"

Helen was startled from her internal monologue of panic and desperation by a voice that reminded her of Al Pacino. It was a voice that had endured significant wear and tear from too much whiskey and too many cigarettes. She looked to her left and saw a man grinning at her through crooked, nicotine-stained teeth. No, grinning was the wrong word. This bastard was leering at her.

"Excuse me?" she asked.

"You're looking for Baby Gumdrop," he rasped as he licked his cracked lips. "I know that look. I've seen it a thousand times this week."

"Is that right?" Helen asked, humoring the man for reasons she couldn't fully comprehend.

"You bet," he said, shoving his hands into the pockets of his threadbare Dickies. "So do you want Baby Gumdrop or not?"

"I do but she's not here and I've got a two-hour drive home, so if you'll excuse me…"

"I've got one left," the man interjected, catching Helen off-guard.

She stared at him in disbelief. This guy had Baby Gumdrop? It didn't even look like he owned a toothbrush.

"Do you want it or not?"

Was this guy kidding? Of course she wanted it.

"You've got Baby Gumdrop?"

The man nodded, his leering grin growing even wider.

"Where is it?" Helen asked, hoping she didn't sound too eager.

"My car," he said, nodding his head toward the exit.

And there it was. The catch. But Helen wasn't ready to give up just yet.

"So go and get it," she said. "I'll wait."

"No way," the man replied shaking his head. "Like I said, there's a thousand parents looking for this thing. Somebody sees me with it, they're liable to tear me apart. Or make me a hell of an offer."

This got Helen's attention. He was absolutely right. The most Helen could offer him was a hundred bucks, which was a pittance compared to what other people would inevitably offer him.

"What about putting it in a bag and then meeting me just inside the entrance?" she suggested.

"I ain't settin' foot in this place with that thing," the man said, holding his ground. "You want the thing, you come out to my car."

Helen knew it was a terrible idea but she was desperate. And this bastard knew it.

"All right," he said when she didn't respond right away. "Good luck finding one on your own then."

He started to walk away and Helen felt her only remaining chance to give her daughter the happiness she deserved slowly melting away.

"Where's your car?" Helen called out, hoping she wasn't making the biggest mistake of her life.

"Parked near the hundreds of other cars at this place," he replied. "If I was gonna try somethin' unsavory, it wouldn't be at a crowded mall at Christmas time."

And God help her, but that actually made a lot of sense.

"Lead the way," she told him.

As Helen exited the mall, she heard a cacophony of screaming voices inside her head. They belonged to her mother, girlfriends, teachers, and every other sensible woman who had been an important part of Helen's life.

"Following a strange man to his car?" they shrieked at her. "Are you insane?"

Helen decided she probably was. But wasn't that the effect Christmas had on everybody? And she was playing it safe, or at least as safe as the circumstances would allow. She stayed behind the man a good ten feet and had her hand wrapped tightly around the can of pepper spray she kept inside her purse. Still, the chorus of those far more rational than her continued to sound in her head unabated.

"This guy has Baby Gumdrop like you've got a Bentley, turn back now!"

Helen tried her best to repress these voices but they wouldn't go away. Probably because they were right. Finally, another voice emerged. It belonged to the kid. And her voice managed to drown out everyone else because the kid and her happiness were the only goddamn things that mattered to Helen right now.

"Mommy," the eager voice chirped inside her head. "Does that man really have Baby Gumdrop? And are you going to get her for me?"

Damn right I am, Helen thought, more determined than ever to see this thing through to the end. And even if it was bogus, at least she could say she had tried everything, even risking rape in a mall parking lot. But she was fairly positive it wouldn't come to that.

Pretty sure, anyway.

The snowfall had subsided somewhat as they went outside but it was still harsh enough for Helen put on her gloves and hat. As they continued walking past the rows of cars, Helen imagined the smile on the kid's face when she presented her with the doll Christmas morning. She saw the kid carrying it everywhere, a testament to Helen's unconditional love and dedication. Thinking about all that was almost enough to offset the frigid cold and dicey nature of her current situation. Almost.

Helen maintained her distance and held onto the pepper spray as they reached the darkened loading dock behind Macy's. She stopped, suddenly feeling very scared and very stupid. The whole thing had been bogus. And part of her knew that but she had soldiered on anyway. What had seemed like determination just a few moments ago suddenly seemed careless and sloppy.

"Why are you stopping?" the man asked, turning around to face her.

"Where are you parked?"

"Behind the loading dock," he said. "Between the merchandise I'm hauling and the fact my car got clipped the last time I was here, I wanted to park it somewhere safe. It's right up here."

He started to walk again but Helen refused to move.

"It's fifty feet away," the man said with a shrug. "But if you want to give up now."

"I'll stay here where it's lit," she said, pointing up at the street light. "Get it from your car and bring it over to me."

"Fair enough," the man said as he headed for an old green pick-up truck. Helen watched as he took a set of keys out of his pocket and unlocked the passenger door. He briefly rummaged around inside before emerging with a bright pink box. It was Baby Gumdrop. Helen couldn't believe it. The scummy creep *had* been telling the truth.

He walked over to her with the doll and held it out to her. It was in pristine condition with Baby Gumdrop smiling vacuously at Helen through a sheet of transparent plastic.

"How much?" Helen asked, her voice quavering and on the verge of tears. "I've got a hundred bucks on me. Please say that's enough because...."

She trailed off and put a shaking hand on the box as if trying to assess whether or not it was real. She felt smooth painted cardboard when she put her hand to it. It was real and if it was making her this happy, the kid was likely to shit a solid gold brick.

"The money's fine," the man answered, gently pulling the box away from her. "But how badly do you want it?"

"What do you mean?" she asked as dread began to creep around inside her like a hungry spider.

"I mean I see the look on your face and I think there's a woman who's willing to do just about anything to get this doll. Even beyond money."

Helen wanted to puke. Was this lecherous bastard asking her to do the unthinkable for a fucking toy?

"Ain't no thing," he said with a shrug. "You'd be my third in the last two days. And those other women were all smiles when they left."

Helen wanted to kick the asshole in the nuts and blast him with her pepper spray but then she thought of the kid and the smile that was waiting for her on Christmas day when she opened up her very own Baby Gumdrop.

Helen took a deep breath as the man stared at her expectantly.

It was like she told herself over and over.

She would do anything for the kid.

And tonight was going to be no exception.

"Baby Gumdrop!"

The squeal was loud enough to be heard two towns over and high enough to shatter crystal (not that Helen owned any). Under ordinary circumstances, Helen would have found it irritating but on this day, it sounded like music to her. The kid ran over and hugged Helen as tightly as her little arms would allow. Helen hugged her back and kissed her on her top of her head.

"Merry Christmas, baby!"

The kid released her hold on Helen and returned to Baby Gumdrop, ripping into the packaging with complete abandon. Within seconds, Baby Gumdrop was freed from her cardboard prison and resting in the kid's loving arms. Helen could think of no better fate for either party. She sat back and had a sip of red wine as she thought about the man who made it all possible. Although their time together had been brief, Helen wasn't exactly proud of what she had done but desperate times called for desperate measures. Even with that in mind,

Helen had no intention of ever telling anyone what she had done to get the kid Baby Gumdrop. She wanted it to be a secret that would stay buried forever.

Just like him.

The Woman in the Woods

It was the fall of 1989 when I almost died at the hands of the woman in the woods. I was eleven years old and in the sixth grade. I wasn't the most popular girl but I still made a point to be nice to everyone. It was a lesson my mother had instilled in me early on but it had its downsides. At that time, said downside was a boy named Frankie Douglas. Frankie was an odd, twitchy boy with cowlicked red hair that looked like it hadn't been washed in years. He wore oversized glasses with smudged lenses and I never saw him dressed in anything other than blue sweatpants and a faded red Buffalo Bills t-shirt. He had a habit of disrupting class, which made the teachers and students dislike him in equal measure. I was the only one who was nice to him and as a result, he had developed a bit of crush on me.

School was ending that fateful day in early October when he came up to me. I was at my cubby hole gathering my books and coat.

"Hi, Amber!" I heard him say in that strange, hoarse voice of his.

I turned around to see him staring at me with a lopsided grin that in retrospect was actually kind of cute.

"Hi, Frankie," I said with my best attempt at a friendly smile.

"I got you a present!" he continued, his goofy grin growing even wider.

I immediately became uncomfortable. Other than cards on Valentine's Day, I had never gotten a present from a boy. The fact it was from Frankie made it all the more awkward.

"You did?" I asked, hoping it was his weird attempt at a joke.

He nodded and took out a small blue packet.

"What is it?" I asked, hesitant to take it.

"It's sneezing powder!" he announced as if he had just given me the keys to a new car. "You take it and blow it in somebody's face and they start sneezing like crazy!"

He doubled over laughing and I could only look at him in confusion. I didn't get boys then and you could argue with a divorce under my belt and a string of failed relationships that I still don't.

Since I was eager for this to be over, I took the packet from Frankie and politely thanked him. He was out the door after that and through the window, I could see him chasing birds before running down the street at full speed. Relieved, I pocketed Frankie's gift and gathered up the rest of my belongings. I never saw Frankie again after that day. And thirty years later, that remains my biggest regret because as it would turn out, I'd owe him my life.

Mom picked me up in front of the school like always. Most of the other kids got to walk home but for me, that was strictly forbidden. This was during the height of the infamous Satanic Panic and as I was a little girl with blonde hair and blue eyes, that made me an ideal target. It's silly looking back at it now and even sillier when you consider what an intelligent woman my mother was but as Dad had left us four years earlier, I was all she had.

Her fear of me being whisked away by Satanists also meant I was never allowed to be home alone for any given length. Most of the time I went to Mrs. Bailey's house and given the choice between going there and being sacrificed, I probably would have opted for the latter. Mrs.

Bailey was an ancient woman whose house smelled like Windex and mothballs. She had a dozen cats (all of them mean) and she never let me pick what we watched on television. She favored boring soap operas and always fell asleep before they ended. I made the mistake of turning the channel one time and she immediately woke up and nearly tore my head off. Suffice to say I never made that mistake again.

Today was going to be different, though. Mrs. Bailey was unavailable and my babysitter was going to be Danielle Ashford, the granddaughter of Mercedes Ashford, a rather famous citizen of our little town. While her name suggested a glamorous Golden Age Hollywood actress, Mercedes was something of an eccentric who resembled a bag lady more than she did Rita Hayworth. She lived in a ramshackle house about two blocks away from us. Despite her shabby appearance and dwelling, she was rumored to be extremely wealthy but most people avoided her just the same. Mom was the exception. She always made a point to engage with Mercedes whenever she ran into her. All things considered, the two had quite the rapport. It was Mercedes who had volunteered Danielle as a babysitter. That was curious considering neither of us had ever met or even seen the girl. She was homeschooled and never seemed to leave the house. While I was a little nervous about being left with someone related to Mercedes, I was also intrigued. I had never spent extensive time with an older girl before.

When we got home that afternoon, I plopped down in front of the television while Mom got ready for the evening. She ran her own catering business in those days and was considered the best in town. I got to accompany her on a lot of jobs but as this function was serving alcohol, she deemed my presence to be inappropriate. The event was being put on by the town's lawyers and I knew my mother wasn't happy about it. The men tended to get a bit handsy after a few cocktails.

She had a staff of six who all wore the same matching white shirts and black pants but as it was Mom's company, she tended to dress as if she were a guest at the event. Going to work with her was worth it just to see her engage with the town's movers and shakers. Everyone loved my mother and her success as a caterer came largely as a result of that.

Mercedes' granddaughter was set to arrive at 3:30 and at five minutes before, Mom came in to reiterate the rules for the evening. I only half paid attention, as the rules were the same as always and I never had any problem following them. The doorbell rang just as Mom finished her spiel and she was pleased to see that Danielle was right on time.

As she got up to the answer the door, my attention shifted slightly from the cartoons I was watching. By this point, I was a little bit excited. I had always viewed teenage girls as the pinnacle of culture and fashion, so to say I was disappointed when I first laid eyes on Danielle would be an understatement.

She was a pale, lanky girl with frizzy hair that had been haphazardly crammed into a scrunchie that sat on top of her head. She was wearing an oversized navy sweater over a faded denim skirt. Her sweater was badly pilling and her lint-covered tights bagged at the ankles. Worse yet were her brown loafers, which looked ready to disintegrate at any given moment.

But true to form, Mom treated her like an old friend. She told

Danielle to help herself to anything in the fridge before handing her a twenty to order us pizza for dinner.

"Don't let this one hog the television all night!" she admonished, addressing me more than she was Danielle.

After laying out a few more instructions and giving me a quick kiss on the check, Mom was out the door, her heels clacking on the front walkway as she made her way to her car. After she was gone, Danielle's first order of business was to rip the remote out of my hands and change the channel.

Rude as it was, I kept my mouth shut. I still didn't know what to make of this strange girl. After flipping through about a dozen channels, she stopped on HBO, which happened to be showing *Evil Dead II*.

"Fuck yeah!" she said. The look on her face suggested she was challenging me to protest her bad language and the movie we were watching. The joke was on her, though. I loved horror movies.

As Bruce Campbell spent the next ten minutes chainsawing his way through demons and deadites, Danielle brought out a metal nail file and began lazily scraping it across her fingernails. Considering how sloppy the rest of her appearance was, I found this to be yet another odd aspect of a girl who seemed to have plenty of them. What made it even more curious was the fact her nails looked like they had been bitten down to the nubs. Once she lost interest in that, she turned her attention back to me.

"What do you think of this movie?" she asked.

I could tell by her tone that she thought she already knew the answer. I was all too happy to disappoint her.

"I like it," I replied. "But the first one is scarier."

Danielle's cocky expression faltered but she wasn't ready to throw in the towel just yet.

"You watch these types of movies?" she asked with a tinge of disbelief in her voice.

"All the time," I answered honestly, barely able to contain my glee.

"And your mom lets you?"

"I have my own television, so I mostly watch them in my room."

Danielle considered this and then a smile formed on her face that bore an uncomfortable resemblance to the Grinch. She came over and knelt down next to me.

"So you like scary things?" she asked.

"I love them," I said but my confidence was waning. Danielle had something planned and not knowing what it was made me nervous. She slid forward on her knees to get closer to me.

"What if I told you I knew about something that was scarier than anything in these movies?"

A bold claim but one that still managed to get my attention.

"How scary is it?" I asked.

She got even closer to me and I didn't like that. She smelled like bug spray.

"So scary you'll piss your little corduroy pants," she proclaimed with a wrinkle of her nose.

Feeling defensive, I sat up until I was almost eye level with her. It had been several years since I had, to use her phrasing, pissed my little corduroy pants.

"What is it?"

"I can't really explain it," Danielle said with a shrug. "I'd have to show it to you."

Now my interest was really piqued. What could it possibly be?

"Feel like taking a walk?" she continued.

I thought about that. While my mom's rules never explicitly stated I couldn't leave the house, it was certainly implied (especially in the throes of the Satanic Panic). Still, the prospect of walking the streets with a teenage girl was too good to pass up, even if she did have bad hair and baggy tights.

We put on our coats and set out but not before I made sure to lock the front door and place the key securely in my back pocket.

"Where are we going?" I asked Danielle as we made our way down the street.

She gave me a decidedly vulpine grin and uttered two words:

"Perkins Forest."

She said it in a way that suggested we were about to enter the gateway to hell. And while it wasn't quite that, it was still pretty damn close.

Perkins Forest bordered the very edge of our neighborhood and when you considered its proximity to the suburbs, it was surprisingly large and dense. It had a handful of trails snaking through it and during the summer months, it was a popular camping and hiking spot. Mom and I had taken our share of hikes through it and while its size was intimidating, it wasn't particularly scary. We had even seen a doe with two fawns the previous July. I wondered what could be so scary about a place that sheltered so much beauty and innocence but admittedly, my experience with Perkins Forest was limited to the trail that was closest to my house. To my disappointment, that's where we headed.

"I know that trail," I said to Danielle, not bothering to hide my displeasure. "There's nothing scary on it."

"We're not staying on the trail," she replied. "What I'm going to show you is nowhere near it."

The nervousness that had begun back at the house was beginning to creep its way up my spine. It was still light out but this was the time of year where the days began to get much shorter. It wouldn't be long before it was dark out and I didn't fancy wandering around a forest at night, especially when we didn't have flashlights. As we got closer, Danielle pulled out a crooked cigarette and lit up, which only served to increase my anxiety. Being eleven didn't generate much wisdom but I knew one thing for sure: Only bad kids smoked.

We reached the entrance of the trail and Danielle looked at me with an eager glint in her eye.

"You ready?" she asked.

I wasn't but I did my best to put on a brave face.

"You bet!" I answered in a voice that was only slightly shaking.

Danielle gave me another vulpine grin and we entered the woods. Our destiny awaited.

It didn't take long for me to fully regret my decision. In addition to my already growing anxiety, it had rained earlier that day and the trail was a mess of wet leaves and mud. Once summer ended, Perkins Forest was mostly abandoned, save for teenagers using it as a party spot on the weekends. As this was a rainy Monday, we pretty much had the place to ourselves. We walked up the trail a few hundred yards before Danielle broke left and made her way through the trees and overgrowth.

"In there?" I asked, unable to hide my trepidation any longer. I was now having visions of poison ivy sticking to my skin while venomous snakes nipped perilously at my ankles.

Danielle turned to me with a look of impatience.

"I told you it was off the trail!"

"How far?" I asked, feeling my stomach churning hungrily for the pizza that should have already been ordered.

"It's really close," she insisted.

"Promise?"

"Promise," Danielle said, holding out her hand. Given how confrontational she had been up to that point, I found this gesture surprising. What was even more surprising was just how warm and confident her grip was when I took her hand. It was just the boost I needed to continue.

We traversed through bushes and stepped over rocks and fallen trees. For a brief period, I was actually happy with our little adventure, at least until I stepped into a large puddle and soaked my shoes and socks.

"I'm wet!" I announced to Danielle as my feet squished with each step.

"We're almost there," she assured me but I was too cold and wet to care. Just as I was about to tell her that I had reached my limit, she stopped and put her hand on my shoulder.

"There it is," she whispered excitedly, pointing her finger directly in front of us.

I looked but saw only trees and waning daylight.

"I don't see anything," I said, letting annoyance creep into my voice.

Danielle slowly lowered her finger and that's when I saw the hole. We got closer and I could see it was about six feet wide by about ten feet deep. Had I the means and know-how to measure it, I'm guessing it would have revealed itself to be a perfect circle. It certainly looked that way to my young eyes and while it was kind of impressive, it wasn't worth suffering wet shoes and an empty stomach for.

"It's just a hole," I said. "What's scary about it?"

"Watch," Danielle whispered. We peered into the hole and saw only wet leaves. In addition to being hungry and disappointed, I was also angry. Danielle wasn't just weird; she was a liar. I badly wanted to give her a piece of my mind but before I had a chance to do so, the ground at the bottom of the hole moved. It was slight at first, barely more than a twitch. I didn't think much of it but then it began to throb and pulsate, rising in waves and decompressing as the mud squelched and the wet leaves scratched against each other. It *was* scarier than anything you'd see in a horror movie. Part of me wanted to run away screaming but another part of me found it strangely hypnotic. I watched as the ground rose and fell in a slow, almost rhythmic fashion. It reminded me a bit of my grandfather, who tended to pass out after too much wine on Christmas Eve.

"Pretty scary, right?" Danielle asked, finally snapping me back to reality.

I wanted to respond but my mouth felt like it was filled with cotton. I gave a quick nod instead and Danielle responded with a triumphant smile. She had successfully scared me and it only took a walk in the woods and a strange hole to do it. But the show wasn't over yet.

"Check this out!" she said as she bent down to pick up a large stick.

She briefly held it over the hole before dropping it down. The stick hit the ground with a muted thud and the movement suddenly ceased. I was ready to pivot and make a run for it when vines shot out of the ground and wrapped themselves around the stick. The vines (if you want to call them that) were obsidian in color and bore a rather strong resemblance to black licorice. They tightened themselves around the stick, stripping it bare before the ground fluttered and opened up. I gasped when I saw what I thought were rows of jagged teeth but as I looked closer I saw it was actually just roots and rocks. Or so I told myself.

There was a grotesque sucking sound as the stick was slowly dragged into the ground. The opening closed around it and within seconds, the stick was gone. The ground was back to being nothing more than a resting place for wet leaves.

"The hole *ate* it," I whispered in a voice that no longer sounded like my own.

"That's right," Danielle said with a smug smirk. "But you know what it really likes to eat? Kids!"

She lunged forward like she was going to push me, causing me to stumble back. For a few horrific seconds, I thought I really was going to fall into the hole but Danielle grabbed my hand and helped me regain my balance. She started braying laughter and at that moment, I hated her. She only stopped when I saw how upset I was. She nervously lit up another cigarette and took a deep drag.

"How did you find it?" I asked. I wasn't quite ready to be friends again but as she was my only way out of the woods, I decided to at least keep things pleasant.

Danielle shrugged and jettisoned smoke from her nostrils.

"I was just out walking by myself and I found it."

I saw something in her eyes that I didn't understand then but do now: Danielle was a lonely girl.

"Can we go back now?" I asked. I had seen everything I needed to.

"Sure," Danielle said. "First we'll get you into some dry clothes and then we'll order pizza. I'll even let you pick what we watch on TV. How does that sound?"

I thought it sounded wonderful. We started back for the trail when a shrill voice filled the forest.

"Stop right there!"

We slowly turned around to see a woman standing behind us. She was, without question, the most striking woman I had ever seen. She had a head full of flowing hair that was so white it was almost blinding. She was dressed in black from head to toe and had a velvet frock wrapped around her shoulders that fell to her ankles. What was most striking were her eyes. They were the color of emeralds and like the hole she was standing in front of, they had a hypnotic quality that made me drowsy. It was only when she spoke again that I was fully at attention.

"What are you doing here?"

She seemed genuinely puzzled by our presence. Didn't she know the forest was public property?

"We were just out walking," Danielle answered nervously. "But we're going home now. Come on, Amber."

She put her hand on my back and started to lead me away when the woman stepped in front of us and blocked our path. We tried to push past her but the woman refused to move. She shoved Danielle to the ground as a cruel smile formed on her crimson lips.

"What the fuck is your problem?" Danielle shrieked as she got to her feet. Her clothing had been transformed into a Rorschach pattern of wet spots and mud. Seeing her so dirty and frightened made my chest hitch. The tears weren't there yet but they would be soon.

"You can't leave," the woman said. Her voice had dropped several octaves but the commanding tone remained and confirmed our worst fear: We weren't going anywhere.

"Yeah?" Danielle asked as her own tears began to emerge. "Try and stop us and we'll fucking...we'll..."

She trailed off and the woman waited for her to go on, her emerald eyes dancing with mockery and scorn. Danielle's lip began to quiver. She didn't have any ideas and the woman knew it. Her only shot was one final plea and it was as pathetic as you could get.

"Please?"

It was almost too quiet to hear and was more of an exhalation than a word. The woman regarded us with her brilliant green eyes and for a moment, I was delusional enough to think that she was actually going to let us go.

She bent over in a way that suggested she was going to tie her shoes but instead grabbed me and Danielle by our arms and hoisted us

up like we were sacks of dirty laundry. We immediately began
screaming as hot tears streamed down our cheeks. The woman's face
never faltered and her grip never wavered. Instead, she began to slowly
walk us toward the pit. And by that point, I definitely saw it as a pit. A
hole suggested something innocuous and this thing was anything but
that.

We reached the very the edge and as terrifying as it was, we didn't
struggle. If we did that and managed to loosen the woman's grip, we'd
end up falling in the pit. The only thing left to do was beg for mercy
and both of us already knew that this woman had none of that to spare.

She turned her body so I was now over solid ground. That gave me
a shred of relief but then I watched as the woman held out her right
hand with Danielle's arm still firmly clasped inside it. Danielle's feet
dangled over the pit and she was screaming for the woman to let her
go. Given our current circumstance, I thought her words were rather
poorly chosen and as if to confirm that, one of Danielle's shoes slid off
and fell into the pit. There was a brief a sucking sound as her loafer
disappeared, prompting more screaming and crying from both of us.
Danielle started to say something about her grandmother having
money when the woman dropped her. Danielle let out a brief shriek
before hitting the ground below with a loud thud. The woman brought
me closer so I could see what was coming next. Danielle looked up at
us, her face frightened and disoriented. It was as if she had forgotten
where she was but then realization set in. She immediately tried to
climb out but only came away with handfuls of mud. Black vines shot
out of the ground and wrapped themselves around her, digging into
her flesh and drawing blood. It streamed down the vines and dripped

onto the ground, which began trembling in what I can only describe as anticipation.

"Amber!" Danielle screamed in equal parts pain and terror.

I could only watch helplessly as she was pulled toward the center of the pit. The ground slowly opened up as she got closer, giving me a better look of the teeth that moments earlier were just rocks and roots. There was no deluding myself this time, though. Danielle wasn't just being dragged into the ground; she was being dragged into the maw of a creature previously unknown to mankind or at least one mercifully avoided. As it sucked the rest of her down, her eyes began to close as if she were in a deep trance. She was no longer screaming but her entire body was shaking. The vines continued to tighten around her and I could hear the ghastly sounds of her bones breaking. Her face, amazingly, remained unchanged but even if she was no longer feeling physical pain, the mental and emotional anguish she was in must have been unreal.

As awful as it was to watch, I couldn't look away. The thing I remember most is Danielle's pale hand. Eventually, that was the only thing left of her and it was positioned in a way that still begged for rescue. And as much as I wanted to do just that, I had problems of my own. Her hand was finally sucked down and although I've debated this with myself for the past thirty years, I'm almost positive I heard that horrible thing burp.

What isn't up for debate is that I was in complete hysterics. The woman slowly swung me around and prepared to drop me in as she had Danielle. As delirious with fear as I was, I suddenly remembered Frankie's sneezing powder. I reached into my pocket with my free arm and pulled the packet out. I used my teeth to rip it open and just as the woman was about to dangle me over the pit, I threw the entire thing in her face. It came out as a white puff that briefly hovered in front of her nose and eyes before uselessly dissipating into the wind. For a soul-crushing few seconds, I was convinced Frankie's gift was a hoax and that my fate was now sealed but then I saw the woman tilt her head back and contort her face.

"Ah-choo!"

Unlike her commanding voice, the woman's sneezes sounded like a noise a cartoon chipmunk might make. Under ordinary circumstances, I might have laughed but we were well past that point.

It was five sneezes before she finally dropped me. I landed on the edge of the pit and my left leg dipped briefly inside. I quickly pulled it out and crawled away as the woman's sneezing fit continued. I was almost out of her reach when a vine shot out of the pit and wrapped itself around my ankle. It began to pull me back and I looked around for anything that could serve as a weapon when I saw the dull glint of something metal poking out of the leaves. It took me a second to recognize that it was Danielle's nail file. It had presumably fallen out of her pocket when the woman pushed her down but I didn't have time to think about logistics. I was almost to the edge of the pit again.

I grabbed the nail file and began to stab at the vine. I jabbed myself twice in the leg but hit the vine enough times to cause it to spurt a thick, foul-smelling liquid that managed to burn through the pant leg of my cords where it sizzled against my skin. As excruciating as that was, my work wasn't done yet. It took four good hits for it to let me go and my timing proved to be fortuitous. The woman was still in the throes

of her sneezing fit and it was only after I began to run that she was able
to give chase.

"Stop!" she roared as I ran as fast as my little legs could carry me. I
had no idea where I was going but knew I had to keep moving even as
a painful stitch formed in my side. There were several times where I
felt her fingertips brush the back of my coat and as impossible as it
seems now, that only made me run faster. I eventually reached the edge
of the woods where I could see the hazy orange of the streetlights
through the trees. With one final Herculean push, I sprinted like an
Olympian and burst through the tree line before falling into a patch of
tall, wet grass. I lay splayed out on my back as a brilliant rainbow of
colored dots danced in front of my face. I half-expected to see the
woman looming over me but as I slowly sat up and looked around,
there was no sign of her. I was unsure of where I had lost her and had
no desire to find out. My legs felt like overcooked spaghetti but I
managed to get to my feet and run the three blocks to my house. Once
I was safely inside, I locked every door and window I could find before
taking refuge under my bed.

The only thing left for me to do was weep.

I was still hiding when Mom returned home an hour later. The
event had been a bust and she got to go home early, which suited her
fine as she got paid the same amount and didn't have to worry about
being groped once the men got drunk. I heard her kick off her heels as
she called for me and Danielle. I listened as she wandered around the
house, calling for us as her voice gradually grew more panicked and
agitated. It wasn't until I saw her stockinged feet enter my room that I

finally crawled out from under my bed. She took one look at my dirt-streaked face and clothing and gasped.

"Amber! What happened?"

I could only stare at my horrified mother in response. And when she asked me where Danielle was, I didn't have an answer.

In the weeks that followed, there were a number of stories that circulated around about what had happened to me and Danielle. Not surprisingly, the most prominent one was that we had been kidnapped by Satanists and it was only by some miracle that the little blonde-haired girl with blue eyes managed to escape. I was diagnosed with deep trauma and after the police realized they weren't going to get anything out of me, they left me alone. The search for Danielle stretched over three states but no one ever found any sign of her. Why would they? There was nothing left of her to find. Mercedes, who was already in failing health, died shortly after that. Counting my mother, her funeral had less than a dozen attendees and if there was a fortune, it certainly didn't go to anyone in town.

It was two months before I returned to school. To my relief, the teachers and students mostly stayed out of my way. I'm sure they all had questions but none of them ever built up the courage to ask them. My first order of business was to talk to Frankie but I learned his family had moved away during my absence. The rest of the school had already forgotten about him but he's never left my thoughts. In the years since I've tried to track him down but it's been to no avail. It's almost like he never existed in the first place.

Mom and I did our own moving a few years later and once I

reached adulthood, I went even further west and ended up in San Francisco as a software engineer. It's not the most exciting job but it pays well and I get to wear jeans to work. I turned forty last year and save for a sag here and a wrinkle there, it's been about the same. I'm single and planning on the staying that way for the foreseeable future. The only time that decision feels regrettable is late at night when I'm lying in bed with the sounds of the city humming pleasantly around me. It's during these moments of tranquility when I'll see the woman standing in front of me, her eyes burning like green flames. She's not actually there, of course. The sightings are nothing more than my imagination working overtime but, in those moments, I'm eleven years old and scared beyond belief.

I sporadically use the internet to check on my hometown and in the last thirty years, there have been three disappearances in Perkins Forest. Rescue teams scoured every acre of the place with dogs but found no trace of the victims. There have also been no recorded sightings of a mysterious woman presiding over a pit with a hungry monster at the bottom. I've often wondered how Danielle managed to find it on two separate occasions while professionals with trained animals found nothing.

But then I remember how strange Danielle was. I also realize just how strange I am. It may not seem like a big deal these days but a little girl who preferred horror movies to Barbie was downright taboo in the 80s. Maybe Frankie's attraction to me wasn't because I was nice to him but because he saw in me a kindred soul. Perhaps the strange things in this world only make themselves known to the strange people. If that's true, I fully expect the woman to pay me a visit someday.

And when she does, I'll have the sneezing powder ready.

A Life in Nightmares

Last night I was attacked by a team of wild boar. Despite my best efforts to escape, the vile things caught me and ripped at me with their jagged, blood-stained tusks. The night before that, there was a rabid dog trying to get into my home. Last week, I ran afoul of a swarm of very large and very angry bees. I've been on something of a wild animal kick as of late and I don't know why. I've never been able to make sense of my nightmares and I'm too old to start now. I began having them nightly when I was a child and it was as frightening and traumatic as you'd expect. My father insisted it was just a phase but my mother took me to see several psychiatrists. Things were a little different in those days and rather than attempting to discuss the issues I might have at length, I was prescribed medicine that made me very tired but did little to dissuade my nightmares. Eventually I learned to accept them and they became just another part of my existence. They don't really bother me anymore and they certainly don't scare me. Now I know what you're thinking—how can they be nightmares if they're not scary? Because, frankly, it feels misleading to call them 'dreams'. Dreams suggest something enjoyable or at least innocuous. The images I endure every night are far from enjoyable and innocuous. Zombies, nuclear war, serial killers, and drowning (just to name a few) aren't things most people aspire to encounter in their lives. But they're what I encounter every time I go to sleep. And the older I get, the less of that I need. That's one plus of being elderly. I haven't found many others.

After I wake up each morning, I go outside and bring in the paper. Then I fix myself coffee, toast, and a poached egg for breakfast. Once I've finished that elaborate feast, I sit down and record the previous evening's nightmare in my journal. As I've been doing this for the better part of sixty years, I have a lot of journals. I don't always remember the nightmare though. Sometimes I'll wake up and whatever it was has been reduced to fleeting vapors. On those days, I simply write 'Don't remember'.

Then I'll spend a few hours reading. Three days a week I like to do a few laps in the community pool. Once the sun goes down, I have dinner and then I go to bed. That's my life.

Not bad, all told.

It seems my subconscious is no longer interested in wild animals. Last night I was on a golf course that I used to frequent with my friend Stan. A heart attack claimed him three years ago and I haven't golfed since. This particular golf course was one of the nicest ones in the state but you wouldn't know it based on my nightmare. In addition to dodging softball-sized hail, I also had lightning to contend with. It may seem comical, like that scene in *Caddyshack*, but this lightning blackened the earth when it struck. I could practically feel the heat and smell the ozone it produced. Couple that with the hail and fierce winds and you have a thoroughly unpleasant experience. Still, given my nightmares now number into the tens of thousands, it wasn't especially memorable. There was one strange detail, though. I spent most of the nightmare running toward a club house that always managed to stay far away, no matter how far or fast I traveled. Standing next to the clubhouse was a figure dressed all in white. I couldn't see them well enough to determine age or gender but they had what appeared to be a veil covering their face. For as nonsensical and surreal as dreams are, the figure seemed strangely out of place.

I don't quite know what to make of it.

The mysterious figure returned last night, watching me while I sat trapped inside a burning car. The figure was much closer this time, close enough that I could see the outline of a head through its veil but no detail beyond that. I still have no clue why this is happening. Is this Death's way of saying it's coming for me? Or is the universe telling me I have unfinished business to take care of? I don't know about any of that but I do know one thing:

It's starting to scare me.

It's three a.m. and I'm wide awake. As you've probably guessed, the figure was in my nightmare again. The porcelain dolls my wife collected came to life and attacked me. Since I only kept those ugly things to honor her memory, I found this nightmare to be rather cruel. I used to tease her all the time about how creepy and hideous they were, and in response, she would just buy more. By the time she died, she had about thirty of them, all of which I store in the spare bedroom. That these mementos of my wife and her wry sense of humor have been perverted by my nightmares angers me. I like to think that under normal circumstances, my subconscious would have repressed this terrible ordeal but the presence of the mysterious figure ensured it stayed at the forefront of my memory. This time they were standing outside my bedroom window, no small feat considering my bedroom is on the second floor. As the dolls began to attack, the figure leaned forward and put its hands on the glass, as if it were spectating an exciting sporting match. It relished in seeing me suffer. I won't be going back to bed tonight. I'm going downstairs to fix myself coffee, which I'll be generously enhancing with my old friends Jack and Jim.

How I've missed them.

I woke up with a bit of a hangover this morning. The good news is that I didn't have another nightmare, or maybe I did and just don't remember. That seems unlikely, as even when I forget the nightmares, there's still the faintest traces of them in my memory. None of that today.

And that's fine with me.

Demons held an orgy in my house last night. The place I've lived in for almost fifty years. There have been nightmares that have taken place in my home before but this was the first time it actually felt defiled. I went into the living room after finally rolling out of bed at ten and could only see those horrid things writhing against each other, their bodies coated in blood, slime, and God knows what else. The figure was there, of course. Watching, enjoying, and motioning for me to do the same. Part of me is considering leaving the house for a few hours but the outside doesn't look any more inviting than this once peaceful place.

Perhaps I'll just go back to bed. Unusual for me, as I normally don't sleep during the day.

Can such a thing be done without nightmares?

The answer to that question is 'No' because nothing is sacred anymore, at least not according to my nightmares. My grandmother's house had a beautiful old tree with a tire swing hanging from it. Some of my fondest childhood memories involve that very spot. I know for a fact that none of my nightmares have taken place there. It's a memory that's too pure and perfect to be corrupted. At least until earlier today.

I arrived at the tree to find the mysterious figure standing next to it with my grandmother's severed head in their hand, only she wasn't dead. She proceeded to mock me for gaffes and indiscretions that had occurred years after her death. Some of them I had completely forgotten about, like the time I hit a handicapped boy with a rock, requiring him to get stitches. I was around twelve when that happened. He never dropped the dime on me, either out of fear or due to his limited mental capacity. Regardless, I felt guilty about it for years. It wasn't until I was well into my twenties that the terrible incident had mostly faded from my memory. One thing I hadn't forgotten about was the time I was unfaithful to my wife. My long-dead grandmother had saved that one for last. My one instance of adultery happened on a business trip. I confessed to my wife as soon as I got home and we went to therapy to get past it. And I thought I had but now I find myself overwhelmed with self-loathing and guilt.

After my grandmother finished taunting me with these awful memories, the tree had caught fire and I woke up to the sound of her mocking laughter. Even as I prepare myself a drink, I can still hear it, a ghastly sound that pierces through my ears while it rips apart my mind.

I fear there's no respite from any of this.

I didn't go back to bed last night. I stayed awake with the help of coffee and an old pack of cigarettes I had stashed away in my desk. I quit for good not long after my wife died but puffing away on cigarettes that were almost a decade old is one of the only pleasures I've had lately. I'm tempted to buy another pack but that would entail going out.

And I have no desire to do that.

It's after midnight and I've invited Jack and Jim to join me for another spell and they are more than happy to oblige. I've been up for over twenty-four hours and I know that drinking will only serve to exacerbate my need for sleep.

If that happens, let it be undisturbed.

Please.

Miracles do happen. I managed to stay awake through last night. I'm now on hour thirty-six of no sleep. I have a stomach full of alcohol and a head full of corrupted memories.

Suffice to say, I feel awful.

Hallucinations can occur if you stay awake for too long. I know this to be true because I've seen the figure from my nightmares standing outside my home at various points. It's never for long and they never do anything but stare as they patiently wait for me to fall asleep.

And I have a bad feeling they won't have to wait much longer.

I've found the old .38 that I purchased some years back. My wife hated having a gun in the house but right now, I'm profoundly grateful that I didn't get rid of it.

Something tells me I'm going to need it.

Fifty-five hours without sleep.

Is it possible to feel blessed and cursed at the same time?

I'm seated in my favorite easy chair but I'm no longer alone. The figure is sitting across from me, its veil securely in place. I'm holding a bottle of Jack in one hand and my .38 in the other.

What I want is for the figure to remove the veil and reveal itself to me. Will it be grotesque? Beautiful? A mirror image of my own face? I don't know but I'm only giving it five minutes. Then I'm pulling the plug on the whole damn thing. At this point, I'm not even sure if this is reality or one of my nightmares.

And I'm past the point of caring.

Acknowledgments

It's been a little over two years since the release of my last short story collection. While it feels like yesterday in some regards, it feels like a lifetime in others (so goes the frustrating and enigmatic nature of time). I'm still blessed to have the love and support of my family and friends. Writing comes easier on some days than others but knowing someone besides you will read it makes for pretty good motivation.

For this particular collection, I'd like to thank Martina Moreno for her hard work and immense talent on illustrating the jacket. I'd also like to thank Nick Seibel, Lex Anderson, and Olaolu Jegede for allowing me to read one of these stories out loud and enduring my not-so-dulcet tones.

Thanks also to Chris Finefrock, who's consistently hired me to write scripts, giving me the much-needed income (and by extension freedom) to continue writing these stories. And thank you to John Hartzog for the continued proofreading work.

To my parents Jim and Janel, my sister Jeanne, and anyone who bought these stories separately on Amazon. I hope you don't mind buying them again.

I also want to thank Sirens Call Publications, Kyanite Press, Sanitarium Magazine, and East of the Web for accepting my stories for publication (one of which appears in this collection). Anyone who says they aren't looking for validation as an artist is probably lying. If you're one of those liars (like me), getting somebody else to accept your work and put it out there is a pretty good indication you're on the right track.

It also serves as the aforementioned motivation we all need some days, so to those publications, I say thank you.

In my last collection, I included a short story as a bonus if you were kind enough to read this section. I considered forgoing that here in lieu of brief anecdotes that explain where the stories came from and where I was at when I wrote them (both literally and figuratively). However, if you picked this collection up, I like to think you're just looking for a good story. And I'm happy to meet that expectation. Enjoy this bonus story and most importantly, thanks for reading!

"I'm ready for you."

The voice coming from the other room sounded old and tired. This was going to be even easier than Tony anticipated. He stood up and went through the red plastic beads hanging in the doorway to find a woman pushing sixty seated at a table with an array of tarot cards placed in front of her. Tony had always envisioned psychics as big breasted Eastern European women named Ruby or Esmeralda. This woman, who went by the far less exotic name of Judy, looked even wearier than she sounded. Her dirty blonde hair, sloppily tied in a bun, looked brittle and unwashed. Her face was deeply etched with wrinkles and she was grossly overweight. Tony couldn't imagine listening to her at length when she was this hard to look at, but the misguided rubes she did readings for didn't share that sentiment. They lined up from the time she opened in the morning until she closed at nine o'clock sharp. Never one minute before or after.

Tony knew this because he occupied one of the shithole

apartments that sat across the street from her. Having lost his job three months ago for stealing, Tony was looking for a large influx of cash so he could start over somewhere else. And it seemed Judy had just what he needed to do that. He had spent the better part of a month following her and her equally fat husband around town. The stops they made were pretty basic (grocery store, gas station, dry cleaners) but never once did he see either of them go into a bank. And the small sign hanging in Judy's front window confirmed she only took cash. With the number of people she saw each day, Tony reasoned they had the better part of a king's ransom stashed away.

Once he was sure she didn't have any security cameras, Tony decided the best approach was to act like a client. Breaking in with a ski mask could trigger an alarm and for all Tony knew, Judy and her fat husband might have a gun. He certainly would if he kept that much cash on hand.

It was a Thursday night when he decided to make his move. Unlike most days, there hadn't been many clients and within the last couple of hours, there hadn't been any. He waited until five minutes before she closed to run over and knock on the door. Judy informed him that she wasn't doing any more readings and to come back tomorrow morning. Tony made up a sob story about how he desperately wanted to check on his dead mother but it wasn't until he offered to pay an extra fifty that he was allowed in. After making him wait for another couple of minutes, Judy called him into the parlor. And now here they were, face to face. The con artist and the thief. That's how Tony justified stealing from her because a con artist is all she was. Scamming desperate people with lies and false hope for the tidy sum of three hundred dollars an hour.

As Judy began to shuffle through her tarot cards, Tony wondered where her husband was. He imagined the tub of guts was likely upstairs, asleep in front of the television. He'd certainly be in for a rude awakening when he saw Tony standing in front of him with a gun pointed at his wife's head.

"You wish to speak with your mother?" Judy asked as Tony sat down across from her.

Tony nodded and Judy continued to shuffle through her tarot cards.

"She's very disappointed in you," she continued.

Tony froze. What the fuck was this bitch talking about? His mother wasn't even dead.

"I'm sorry?" he asked. Judy's words were so confusing that Tony had actually forgotten why he was there for a brief moment.

"You've got a lot of nerve," Judy said, her formerly hound-dog eyes now sharp and alert. "Trying to take what isn't yours."

Tony was flummoxed. How could this woman possibly know what he was planning on doing? She wasn't psychic. None of that shit was real.

"I don't know—" Tony started to say before a gunshot rang out. Tony felt himself get struck in the chest, the force of the blast knocking him out of his chair. He gasped for air as Judy stood over him brandishing a freshly-fired pistol.

"You bad man," she said. "You snuck into my home and murdered my husband. Fortunately I was able to shoot you before you were going to do the same to me."

Tony tried to speak but blood was quickly filling the inside of his mouth and throat.

"I should actually thank you," Judy said with a chipper smile that made her formerly weary face look youthful and even attractive. "I've been trying to get rid of my husband for years. And then you came along and provided me with the perfect alibi. Now if you'll excuse me."

Judy went into the next room and made a very convincing 9-1-1 call. She explained that she had found her husband dead in the kitchen and that the man who had killed him was in their parlor, also dead as far as she could tell. After the call ended, she came back into the parlor to ensure that the final part of her plan came to fruition. She didn't have to worry about that. Tony was as good as dead.

"I wasn't kidding about your mother, you know," she told him as everything started to fade. "She is really disappointed in you. And who can blame her?"

Certainly not Tony, who was also rather disappointed. He thought he had a good plan.

Judy's just happened to be much better.

Also available from Michael Subjack:

Midnight Deluxe
(in paperback and eBook)